SLAYER
OF THE SEA

BEAU PETERSON

Appropriate for Teens, Intriguing to Adults

Immortal Works LLC
1505 Glenrose Drive
Salt Lake City, Utah 84104
Tel: (385) 202-0116

ASIN: B07DJ3ZHQX (Kindle Edition)
ISBN: 978-1-7324674-1-5 (Paperback)

For my mother, Lynnette Peterson, who read to me in my youth and whose voice transported me into worlds filled with adventure, sorrow, love, and courage. Thank you, Mom!

PART ONE

Never in my life have I felt despair so crippling it rendered my soul to ash. Not until that ruinous day. Where I had once felt rapture so rich no emperor could comprehend its value, a pit of darkness now grew, like a voracious serpent swallowing whole every joyous memory I ever had.

—Fergus Culkin, captain of the Domnall, *leviathan ship of the first class, personal ship of the king*

CHAPTER ONE

The air was cool and light, the stars glistening blissfully through windows that made up the entire wall of the Cosmos club and restaurant. At a lengthy bar, curved like a faraway rainbow and made of polished wood, Rowan Donchaad sat alone.

Had it been an hour earlier, the view through the hundred panes of stormproof glass that encompassed three of the surrounding walls would have shown an ocean vista unlike anything many folks would ever see—a ship-strewn sea of red and gold fire as Belinos, one of the two suns gracing the sky, followed her partner out of view behind the distant, liquescent, horizon.

Rowan stared aimlessly into his ever-diminishing glass of whiskey. Neat. Ice would have spoiled his spiraling descent into drunkenness. Or at least, delayed it.

Light from hundreds of candles nestled safely in chandeliers thirty feet above the grand hall flickered in rhythm to the sounds of drums, horns, and strings that permeated the air. Musicians and vocalists exercised their top-notch talents while men and women danced to the tempo of their music, twirling and dipping one another with not a care in the world.

Through it all, Rowan could only hear the faint whistle of the wind outside.

Trim the sail, let fall the anchor.

Booths and tables surrounded the grand stage, meals forgotten as patrons in flowing gowns and smart jackets watched, with rapture, the excitement all around them.

Oblivious to their happiness, Rowan's attention was on the glass that spun in his calloused hand. It wasn't his first glass, or his second. It wasn't even his fifth; at least, he didn't think it was. Truth be told, he had no idea how many times the bartender had filled it. Only now the man behind the counter was asking if he wanted something else. A strong tea, was it?

But for all the details he'd seemed to forget, the fact that he could still remember her face told him he hadn't yet drunk enough. He opened his hand, the one not permanently attached to the glass. In it lay a pendant of lightning-struck glass, brilliant blue, like an afternoon sky, rimmed in yellow, polished gold. The blue glass matched perfectly the color of her eyes.

Her eyes.

A lone tear, or maybe a drop of sweat, tracked its way down his cheek only to get lost in a forest of dark brown whiskers. Rowan sniffed and wiped away a second drop with the back of his once-white, linen sleeve, and threw back the last swallow of alcohol.

"Barkeep!" he bellowed. "Another!" His voice echoed conflictingly in the room filled with beautiful music as he held up the empty glass and gave it a wobble. One of the nearby patrons, a woman in yellow satin, glared at him, disapproval evident on her face. Rowan ignored her.

"Enough is enough, Captain," the man behind the counter said. "Please, have the tea? It's imported from the highlands of Pan a'Leigh." The man's apprehensive smile did nothing to convince Rowan to abandon his whiskey.

Rowan eyed the man, or was it *men?* One second, there was only a single person and the next there were two, identical in every way. This was a good sign. First, his vision would go. Next would be his memories. He pinched the bridge of his nose and gave his head a quick shake to clear his vision. "I don't care where it's from," he slurred. "If it's not stored in a barrel and more than fifty years old, I don't want it." The barman rolled his eyes, reaching for an almost-empty bottle of dark brown liquid.

A strong, steady, hand gripped Rowan's shoulder, taking him by surprise, and he turned to see his first mate standing beside him. Aifric was tall—taller than Rowan—with arms built like cannons and a chest so large an entire distillery could be hidden inside it.

"Ahoy, Aifric, my friend," Rowan said, attempting to enunciate his words yet failing badly. "Make yerself at home and pour yerself a drink."

"I didn't expect to find ya here at the Cosmos, Captain," Aifric said, glancing around at the well-dressed people and musicians. He pulled a stool closer and sat with a faint creak of wood. "Thought you'd be at one of the bars down near the docks, see'n as how ya can't stand be'n too far from the sea. I had to shake loose more than one attractive barmaid with brown eyes before come'n all the way up here to find ya. You owe me fer that one, Captain."

Rowan turned away from his friend whose words came more quickly than he was used to. What was that he said about eyes? Brown eyes?

No. Her eyes were blue.

He fingered the translucent pendant again. Light danced off the many planes and angles of the melted glass. The music playing behind him was entirely too upbeat.

"It's like that, is it?" Aifric said, glancing at the pendant. Rowan tensed slightly. Aifric would recognize it, certainly. "Well, I thought as much, I did. Never saw you two grace any other establishment." *He knows.*

"Who?" His hand tightened around the chain. "Oh, right. Yeah, this did be her favorite place," Rowan said, loudly. Competing to be heard over the music was not as easy as it had been earlier. He took a moment to look over the establishment. Everything seemed... fuzzy. "She did love the 'feel' of it, whatever *it* was." Holding aloft the fine gold chain, he tapped the edge of the dangling pendant sending it into a delicate spin. The flash of reflected candlelight would have made him dizzy had he not looked away. A few more drinks should do it. "Never could see what she liked about it," he said, gesturing with a wave that encompassed everything around them.

"Then why'd ya come here, Captain?" Aifric waved over the barman with a glass of water.

Rowan didn't respond.

"If ya hate it so bad, why'd ya come back?" Aifric asked, sipping his water. "Surely, it's not to remember *her*, not with the way you're emptying that glass. If ya wanna forget her, ya don't come to the one place she loved above all else." He glanced over to the musicians and dancers. "A man drinks like that for only one reason."

"Stagnation, Aifric," Rowan slurred, rounding on his friend, a finger directed at the man's face. "Ya know nothing of the hell I do be go'n through. Of course, I don't wanna forget her. I can't forget her, a woman like that. She—" A liveried servant bumped into Rowan's back, trying to make way for a passing couple. The room suddenly began to tilt and Rowan feared he'd be meeting the floor real soon. He threw out his hands and braced himself on the bar until things became right again. *Something's wrong with this place,* he decided. *And what's with that music? Can't they slow it down a little?*

"I beg pardon, sir. Please forgive me?" the serving woman begged. Rowan waved a casual hand, despite the fact he had nearly overbalanced, and the attendant departed with a quick bow. The people here were far too polite. It made him uncomfortable.

Rowan put the servant out of his mind and looked over his shoulder to see the patrons she'd avoided. The woman wore a lengthy gown with shimmering lace and complimented it nicely, in Rowan's opinion, with long, strawberry hair in tight curls. The man wore a long coat of oiled dragon-hide over a bright white linen shirt and sported a hairstyle just as black and oiled as his coat.

"It's not Birgitta yer try'n to forget, is it?" Aifric said. Rowan's stomach opened into a chasm deep enough to consume his darkest doubts and worries, yet for some reason he could never fully push them in. He knew his friend would eventually get to the heart of it all. Aifric was always cleverer than most people realized. "It's her little girl."

Rowan ducked his head, guilt permeating his tired soul. Sweat beaded on his dank, sunbaked, skin.

"Have ya gone to see her yet?" Aifric asked.

Rowan shook his head slightly.

"Stagnation, Rowan," Aifric said, pushing his empty glass away before running his hands through his blonde, shoulder length hair. "She's yer own daughter. How long's it been, eh?"

"A couple of months." Rowan avoided eye contact with his friend. He couldn't stand to see his disappointment.

"Months? We've just spent the last *four* months at sea. Not to mention the month ya spent cooped up in yer ship mourning Birgitta's passing. That's well over a couple months, Rowan," Aifric chided. "It's damn near half a year."

"Look, Aifric, Breanna do be more than capable of

watch'n after Asy while I'm at sea." Rowan sipped his whiskey, holding the burning liquid in his mouth a few seconds longer than normal. "In fact, she's a damn sight better off with Brianna than she ever could hope t'be with her old man. What good can I bring to this arrangement, huh?"

"Ya can't just leave her to be raised by yer sister-in-law, Rowan. The girl, she needs a father." Aifric darted out a hand and took Rowan's whiskey away from him.

In his intoxicated state, Rowan barely even saw Aifric's hand and didn't realize his glass had been whisked away until it was too late. He scowled.

"She needs someone to feed and change her linens. That do be all a baby needs. Not some gender-specific parent." Rowan pulled his hands down his face, rubbing the exasperation from his angry eyes. After a long moment he said, "I don't know how to take care of an infant, Aifric. All I do know is kill'n leviathans and sell'n pieces of them to greedy merchants. I know the sea and the currents, the reefs and the islands. I know the winds and the waves, damn my soul, but I know nothing about raise'n a kid." He snatched his whiskey back and tossed the remainder into his mouth. *Water!* He'd grabbed the wrong glass.

Aifric took Rowan by the shoulders and forced him to face the man. "That's why ya do need to spend time with her. Hold her in yer arms. Look into those eyes and let her get to know her father. Go—"

"Give it a rest, Aifric." Rowan flung the man's arms aside and turned back to the bar. Stars were now sparkling visibly in the night outside the wall of windows. "I've made up my mind on the matter." He grabbed the right glass this time and lifted it to his lips in a wobbly hand, but Aifric ripped it away from him and slid it down the bar, well out of Rowan's reach. Anger began to boil inside. The glass slowed to a stop in front of the man with the oiled leather jacket who looked their way and smiled.

Not too drunk to recognize the dandy looking at them, Rowan tried to lower his voice as he spoke, but the words came out as audible as a gull's screeching. "Now ya done it, Aifric. Who let this idiot in here anyway?" Sighing, he mumbled, "This place is a sinking ship."

CHAPTER
TWO

Had Rowan not been well on his way to being passed out drunk, he'd have been angry at seeing this man in the fancy clothes. As it was, he just felt irritated. Aifric looked up to see him approach and took a wary step back.

He recognized him too.

The approaching man's eyes were locked onto Rowan's.

"Is that you, old friend?" the dandy asked, a smirk adorning his powder-white skin.

"Doubtful," Rowan slurred, "Didn't think ya had any friends left, Lieutenant Alby."

"Lieutenant *Commander*, actually," the newcomer said, running his hands down the pressed leather jacket. "Oh, don't worry. I won't arrest you. And please call me Cassidy, Rowan. It hasn't been that long since we last saw each other." The barkeep handed Cass a glass of clear liquid.

"Lieutenant Commander, eh?" Rowan said with a skeptical frown. "All these years later and yet still not a Commander?"

The man flinched and the air hung thick at the barbed comment, shutting out the merriment of the Cosmos' patrons and employees. Rowan knew that comment would strike a nerve. He liked it.

"Is that water, Cass," he asked winking at the man's glass, "or are ya still drinking all the women's gin?" It was a lame attempt to put the man down, and he knew it as soon as the words muddled past his lips. Had he been sober he would have come up with a much nastier quip.

"Oh, Rowan," Cass said with a pitying smile. "Still bitter after all these years. I really don't know why you've held onto your anger." He reached across the distance between them and flicked the lapel of Rowan's brown, wrinkled, evening jacket and grimaced. "You're clearly doing well for yourself. Even if the attire doesn't reflect it."

"Yeah?" Rowan asked. "Better this jacket than that face. Am I right, Aifric?" he laughed. Aifric didn't respond, just a slight lift of an eyebrow.

"Make your pathetic jokes, if need be, Rowan," Cass said. "Get it out of your system so the next time a ship goes down you can help *save* the crew instead of drinking and joking your way down with them. Your wife would've appreciated that, I'm sure."

Blinding hot rage blossomed inside him like the billow of squid ink. Aifric stepped quickly between the two, clearly sensing Rowan's flaring anger—alcohol definitely brought out the baser part of himself. Rowan slid off his stool and stood somewhat straight, eager to show his former partner what he was made of, but his right knee buckled and he would've gone down had his first mate not been there to catch him.

Cass bellowed with laughter as Aifric helped Rowan back onto his stool.

"Rowan Donchaad," he said, stifling his amusement. "Enough money to buy a palace and yet still a despicable drunk. Looks like I made the right decision all those years ago." He took a measured sip of gin. "Drink up, old friend. It's all you really have left."

The comment took Rowan off guard. Had he really been referring to his wife's death? He looked into Cass's eyes. The cold, emotionless glare he saw told Rowan his presumption had been correct.

"How can ya make light of her death, Cass? How? She was yer sister, after all."

"Was, Rowan," Cass said stoically. "Was. She left that title behind when I found her under *your* covers."

"What was it about me and her together that was so unbearable for ya?" Rowan asked determinably. His fingernails found a shallow crevasse in the bar's surface and he began to pick at it, unconsciously taking out his anger on the counter.

Cass laughed humorously. "Where do I start?"

Rowan slapped his hand down. "How 'bout the part where ya decided to stick me with yer half of the loan? Or how you decided to give up on our dream and go off to join the navy?"

"Questions, Rowan? Don't you ever stop asking questions?" The smug look on Cass's face was almost more than Rowan could bear, but he held his anger in check. "I don't need to answer to you, or your bodyguard," Cass said, giving Aifric a dismissive glance. "I've found a life far better than where you and I were heading. You mock my station? I'll have you know I'll be receiving a new ship soon. One the King just had commissioned. A new war dhow."

"Right. A new war dhow," Rowan laughed. "What a pile of turtle scat. Stagnation, Cass, if you're going to make up stories, make 'em believable." He'd been to the engineer's wharf. No new ships were currently under construction.

Behind them, the music stopped and the hall erupted in applause. A few cat calls and whistles rang out through the club as dancers and musicians bowed to one another. The woman with strawberry curls took the opportunity to move in close to Cassidy and rest a jeweled hand on his arm.

"A new song will be starting up soon, Cassidy," she said, her voice was rich and as sweet as the purest honey. "Won't you dance with me?"

"Do it, Cass," Rowan said. "Dance with yer lady. Twirl her through the air and tell her how yer soon to be the commander of the Kings Flotilla. Tell her how *all* the commanders of *all* the war dhows will bow when they see ya, and kiss yer royal boots when they kneel at yer feet, and how you'll never have to feed yerself or wipe yer own arse ever again."

The flash of light that encompassed Rowan's vision had somehow transported him from his barstool to the polished wood floor. A ringing pressure that hadn't been there before made his head feel as swollen as a bellows. When he looked up, the world around him spun like a wind mill. It gradually slowed and his vision focused in time to find Aifric physically restraining Cass who was shaking his hand with a pained expression.

Rowan staggered back to his feet, now noticing the complete silence around him. Where was the music? Where were the laughing people? They were all staring at him. Staring at *them*.

"You'll pay for that remark, Rowan." Cassidy jabbed Rowan hard in the chest. Rowan's reflexes were too muddled to see it coming. "As dearly as I can manage, you'll pay."

"Didn't I already?" Rowan asked, feeling the puffy skin around his eye. *Stagnation, that swelled up fast.*

"Not a chance," Cassidy said.

The woman with the lacey gown was pulling on Cassidy's arm. "Come, Cassidy. Come away from this *landsman*," she said disgustedly. The look on her entitled face reminded

Rowan of the time he suggested to Birgitta that they should serve fresh roe at their wedding.

"Take her advice, Cass. If'n ya have a brain in yer swollen head," Aifric jeered, shooing him off like a pesky mosquito.

"This isn't over, Rowan," Cassidy said, straightening his expensive jacket. "As far as I'm concerned it will never be over."

"Thanks for the warning, *Lieutenant*," Rowan replied, getting in one last jab at Cassidy's *lowly* position.

Three strangers appeared suddenly—two men in uniform and a woman dressed as elegantly as any in the club, in a tight satin corset, and a black velvet vest that hung open to show a high neckline of finely embroidered lace. Her skirt was of pale blue and reached all the way to the floor. Their appearance seemed a bit sudden to Rowan, but then again, he was drunk.

The men were enormous and their uniform coats were of dark green and gold trim. They held polished clubs in calloused hands. Looking closer, Rowan realized he knew them. Well, maybe not the men, but he definitely knew the woman.

"Kingsman body guards, Declan?" Rowan drawled. The woman owned the club and had always treated Rowan better than fair. "After all those years defy'n these royal buffoons, you've finally sold out to 'em, have ya?"

"Don't patronize me, Rowan," Declan replied with a tolerant smile. She rested her hands on slender hips as she wrested his irritation with her calm demeanor. "You're welcome to return to my establishment, but tonight you've overstayed your welcome." Her smile became somewhat sorrowful. She and Birgitta had been quite close.

"Then why the guards?" he asked, pointing a wobbly finger at the men three feet away from him.

"Just a precaution," she said, glancing at them. Her voice

was rich, smooth, and somewhat calming and put Rowan further at ease. That voice, in part, made her an effective manager. That, and she kept this place the kind of establishment other women would want to go. And wherever women were, men tended to appear.

"Captain, I believe it's time," Aifric said, turning Rowan away from the group of men. To Declan, he said, "I'll come back and settle the captain's bill with ya later, Ma'am, if'n that's ok with you?"

"That's fine, Aifric," Declan said understandably. The club manager waved to the band that was watching anxiously from a safe distance. Instruments were expensive, not to mention rare, and a silent instrument made no money. Instantly, music began to play and the attention of the patrons returned to the performers.

Without a sideways glance, Rowan and his first mate made for the twenty-foot, copper-trimmed doors and exited onto the balcony. Behind them, Rowan heard Cass's familiar laughter cut off as doors slammed shut behind them. Who got the better of the other in that exchange was impossible to tell, but that haunting laughter made him want to punch a wall. Or better yet, a face.

All sounds of merriment were gone and just the night welcomed their presence. The air was cool and brisk, but not uncomfortable. Night bugs chirped and buzzed from the generous foliage around them. As they walked to the wide stairway of intricately carved wood leading down to the boardwalk, Rowan cursed the fact that his drunken state had diminished.

Her eyes returned to the forefront of memory.

Tiny, delicate, and pure.

Should he go see his baby? Would Asy even remember his face? Breanna would remember. She'd remember and no doubt pummel him for abandoning them. After a few minutes of winding down the ever-curving street, he came to a conclusion.

"Aifric?" Rowan asked. He'd shoved his hands in the pockets of his trousers. Somehow, holding himself tightly together helped him feel somewhat better.

"Yes, Captain?" Aifric quickly replied. He looked at Rowan while they walked, his questioning stare seemed to challenge Rowan. *Be a man. Do what's right by your family.*

"I want ya to take one of the smaller chests over to Breanna for me," he said looking straight ahead. "And don't question my motives, Aifric. I'm in no mood to get punched a second time tonight. Just take her the gold."

"Aye, Captain," he said energetically. "And the child?"

"What about her?" Rowan asked, one eyebrow raised.

"I recommend a gift for her as well."

Too tired to argue with the man, he thought for a moment of something he could give Asy, though what a baby would need a gift for, he didn't understand. It came to him instantly.

"Take the earrings her mother used to wear," he said. It was a great idea. "Yes, the green ones. Maybe when she do be older Brianna can give 'em to her." They were lightning-struck glass just like the pendant—rare and beautiful. "They're in my cabin. I'll get them. Then you can take them to her. We sail at dawn so you'll have to make it quick."

"Dawn?" Aifric asked, missing a step. "You told the men we did have a full week at shore, not five days."

"The ship do be re-supplied," he explained. "We got no *real* reason to stay, and I'd like to get as far away from all this parent stuff as possible. Also, I don't much like being this close to Cass. I'm not afraid of what he'll do. I just don't like being that close to trash."

"Sure, Captain. Sure." Aifric said. "But that means I'll need to make a stop on the way back, if'n you think you can make it back by yerself, that is. I need to grab yer new cabin boy."

"That's right. I almost forgot." *Is the alcohol getting to me, or is my memory start'n to slip?* Probably both. "Yeah, of course I can. I'm not nearly as drunk as I wish I was. What do the lad's name be again?"

"Marek," Aifric said.

"Marek," he paused a moment, thinking. "That's a good name," he decided. "Has he any experience on a leviathan ship?"

Aifric burst out in laughter. "Never so much as held a harpoon. But he's a smart lad and the older of my two nephews."

Rowan frowned. An inexperienced cabin boy was what he had last time.

"Don't worry," Aifric said, slapping a hand on his captain's shoulder. "I'll make sure he holds his own. He's me own blood after all."

Hopefully, he won't wash out like the last one. Probably expected too much outa him. The poor kid had spent more time hiding in the hold, scared to death and puking every fifteen minutes, than he did working. *I'll have to take it easy on the new lad this time.*

"Make it quick," Rowan said. "The night ain't so young." He shook his head a bit and blinked his eyes a few times to clear out the cogs. He'd had a lot to drink tonight. "Oh, and don't ya forget to settle my bill with Declan!" he shouted as Aifric turned and sprinted off back up the street. "She looks nice, but she do be one ruthless son-of-a-whore if ya double-cross her!"

PART TWO

One of the most dangerous and crippling aspects of sea life can be the effects of one's own past. All too often, men and women who experience extreme terror let their haunting fears affect their future choices. Choices that can, if not made carefully, lead them into deeper and deeper waters. Waters that will boil them down to mere husks of who they'd once been.

—Fergus Culkin, captain of the Domnall, *leviathan ship of the first class, personal ship of the king*

CHAPTER
THREE

Rowan stood unsteadily as he watched Aifric hustle down the slat roadway ahead of him, his footsteps loud, hollow, thuds on the worn stonewood planks. His first mate was a good man, probably the best. He was definitely better than any on Manks.

The tall spire-shaped island—crowned by the King's palace nesting atop the uppermost peak—drew the wealthiest of their country's dignitaries, Rowan included.

But wealth never did make for an honest gentleman, and those on Manks were the least gentlemanly of them all. That was one reason Rowan escaped to the sea so often, weather permitting.

Each year, the Downs would bring such incredibly violent wind and rain that it would render any kind of sailing impossible. During those weeks Rowan would shut himself away in his manor and refuse to mingle with the other wealthy inhabitants of the islands for any social event, especially the grand balls thrown by the king.

It was his own ship he was headed for now. His escape from that oppressive world. Aifric had his errands and Rowan had his. He needed to get the *Slayer of the Sea* ready to sail as soon as he could, despite the night that enveloped him.

Torches along the outside rail of the roadway illuminated his path.

This late into the evening, few lifts would be in operation, and he was nowhere near one, not unless he wanted to turn around and go back up the road. After a careful, intoxicated thought, he decided to take one of the rope ladders the youth of the island commonly used.

He stumbled over to the inside lane of the road where the supports were anchored solidly into the side of the spire and watched for gaps between the rock and the road as he walked. He soon found one. It looked large enough to fit a man, but when he pushed aside the verdant growth of vines and damp leaves, no ropes were to be found.

Stagnation, I know there do be one close by.

It was the third gap that finally unveiled a pair of ropes. Rowan sat down and swung his legs over the edge, careful not to tangle his boots in the vines. He felt blindly with his feet until he located the first plank. Rowan gradually allowed his weight to settle on the narrow wooden board. Now would be the best time to find out if the ladder was too weathered to support him. *Boil my hide, am I sober enough to be doing something this stupid?* There was a reason these ladders were only used by children.

But he descended the ladder safely, despite being nearly blind in the darkness. His clothes were soaked in evening dew when he got to the lower roadway. He stopped to take a few breaths and let the pounding in his chest settle to a more normal rhythm. *That's one way to sober up.*

This was the same road as up above, only it had encircled the entire spire to get back to the same point fifty or sixty feet down in elevation. *If only more of the damn lifts were still operational.* Rowan decided to avoid the next set of rope ladders even if it meant an extra half hour of walking.

All along the gently curving road, the scattered shops and

homes that recessed in shallow crevasses became smaller and smaller with signs of disrepair becoming more and more common. The lights were more abundant and the sounds of voices emanated from taverns he passed by.

If there be a lift in operation, it do be here that I'll find it.

Sure enough, he found one not twenty paces away where a boardwalk split off from the main road and meandered into a deep crevasse in the island. He knew this section well. In his younger years Rowan and Cass had practically called the *Flats* home. Some of the best dive-restaurants on Manks were tucked away in here. And, of course, the notorious 'Mickey's Brothel' that claimed the fortunes of sailors for as long as Rowan could remember. *Mickey had to be an old man by now.* The thought set his stomach turning.

"Well, if it ain't Cap'n Donchaad," the lift operator said, smiling around a thick cigar clenched between his teeth as he reached for Rowan's hand. His voice was only one of many. The street was alive with people coming in and out of the restaurants and bars.

"Abandinus preserve me, Barney," he said with relief. "I do be glad to see ya." A soft night breeze set him shivering in wet clothes.

"Yer look'n a little worse fer wear, Cap'n," Barney said, plucking the soggy cigar from his teeth and pointing. "What happened to ya?"

Rowan told him about the ladder, deliberately omitting the more embarrassing parts.

"Never had the stomach fer those blasted things," Barney said tapping away the ash. "Not after the first one come unlashed on me. Thought I was a goner fer sure, I did."

Rowan laughed, knowing all-to-well what he was referring to. He'd felt the same way. "You got this contraption ready, don't ya Barney?" he said grabbing one of the support bars that made up the lift cage.

"Sure do, Cap'n. Just let me rouse old Wilma." He jammed the cigar back in his mouth and scurried over to a large mound about fifty paces down the road. Rowan smiled as he watched. The man ran like a penguin, his steps short and knees nearly locked together.

Barney grabbed a hold of a canvas sheet and pulled, revealing one of the famous cart-turtles this island was famous for. It was a massive beast, with a shell as tall as Rowan's shoulders, and covered in metallic swirls that glistened in refracted candlelight. In the glow of a setting sun, these animals shone like angelic servants.

Barney reached in the shell of the sleeping turtle and, after a moment, pulled his hand back out. A flat brown head covered in loose folds of wrinkly skin soon appeared.

"Go ahead and climb in, Cap'n!" Barney yelled. Rowan did so and waved to the man. The lift cage was big enough for about ten men and Rowan felt the absence of the other passengers. He didn't like these lifts much, though he appreciated their usefulness. If it wasn't on a ship, it wasn't for him.

The cage jostled and a sheen of sweat rose from Rowan's skin. A hollow sensation opened in his gut. The lift shifted again and this time began to sink into the road. The wood planks rose to the level of his knees and peering down the lane, he could see Barney slowly guiding Wilma backwards up the street, a long rope fastened to a harness that encircled her shell. He was being lowered by a turtle.

"Thanks again, Barney!" Rowan shouted as the road began to obscure his view of the man.

"Abandinus watch over ya, Cap'n!" came the returning farewell.

Rowan looked out over the sea as the lift dropped foot by foot in soft, rhythmic bounces. He couldn't see much of the water in the darkness, but he knew it was there. The sound of lapping waves soothed his trepid nerves.

The spire of Manks offered a stunning view of suspended bridges lit by torches as they eagerly stretched out hundreds of feet to grasp onto another spire. To Rowan, they looked like angelic pathways to the heavens.

Two spires breached the sea within his view. There were two more out of sight. All four were connected to Manks by massive bridges. It was a marvel of engineering that fascinated even him. It was what made him want to permanently call these islands his home. Besides, Birgitta was from here and he never did feel a need to uproot her.

Ten minutes later, the cage thumped solidly on the lowest dock of the spire. The fisherman's wharf, it was called. He jumped out of the cage and rang a brass bell mounted to the side of the cage to signal his safe arrival.

The wharfs. This was the part of the island he truly loved. Everywhere he looked, he saw aspects of the life he treasured. Tall, beautiful ships were docked here—their masts bare of sail—with men bustling about offloading cargo.

The *Crest*, a wide fishing vessel, was quite unique. The cabins were built at the bow with a single mast set in the middle of the ship to act more as a stay for the two narrower masts that leaned out over the gunnels that suspended sails like bird wings.

Rowan loved this ship for its ingenuity. With no cabins on the stern, the carpenters were able to construct a large open deck where a massive reel laid horizontally could roll out a giant net the captain could pull behind them as they sailed. When they figured the net was full of fish, they would roll in the net and empty it onto the deck. It was quite genius, really, though their target prey was far from exciting.

In the light of day, large derricks would swing over the ships with holds open to allow cargo to be lifted out or lowered into each one. Men and boys hustled about arranging the cargo onto wheeled carts. Rowan remembered the short time he spent working these docks, connecting the carts into trains and harnessing them to the giant cart-turtles that pulled the trains up the steep winding roads.

That was when he met Cassidy, a boil on a leviathan's backside.

He spied the *Slayer of the Sea*, the nucleus of his world, silent and still. He and Cassidy had designed it with the help of their former captain, Fergus Culkin, before he died. They wanted a ship that could stay out at sea longer than any other, one that could hold twice the amount of cargo, and one that could weather the fiercest storms while laden with ridiculous amounts of leviathan scales.

They attached additional hulls on both starboard and port sides with bridges connecting them like catamarans to the main body of the vessel to give them the extra hold space and allow the ship to ride higher on the water as well as a wider base to keep from tilting too hard in heavy winds.

Rowan inhaled a long breath as though pulling the essence of the craft into his soul. She was a beautiful ship, one of a kind. And best of all, she was his and his only. As furious as he was when Cassidy backed out, he'd now come to appreciate the solitary nature of his ownership.

Another ship caught Rowan's eye. It was a standard vessel about the same length as the *Slayer of the Sea*, new to these parts, and berthed just slightly out of view behind the *Slayer*. He'd met the captain before—a scrawny man named Aohd whose fiery temper was well known.

Rumor had it he was a prominent member of the smuggler's guild, though many dignitaries verbally doubted such a group existed. Rowan knew it to be more than exaggeration. He'd have to ask Aifric if he knew the man.

The sound of shouting caught his ear, and he noticed several of the dockworkers heading for Aohd's vessel. *What in Abandinus' name is go'n on over there?* As he walked closer, he could hear the sounds of excitement coming from the crowd of men.

One worker took control of a loading crane and maneuvered it over the hold of the ship while others called for the dockmaster and several loading carts. *They must have some pretty fancy cargo. I wonder what business he do be in. Imports? Fishing?*

Rowan joined the crowd of men, the screeching sound of taut gears from the loading crane crying out from the strain of a remarkably heavy load. Gasps and murmurs erupted from the onlookers as the cargo became visible.

Rowan raised an eyebrow.

The object was the color of smoke, rigid, and hard as iron with two-foot spikes that rimmed the outside and jutted out over a section covered in greenish blood. The front of the blocky object split into a 'V' exposing row upon row of long, razor-sharp teeth.

It was the severed head of a leviathan.

"Abandinus preserve us," someone muttered under their breath. Rowan saw the person who spoke. She wore a tight cap, a loose vest, and held tightly to a small golden trident as if for protection.

Low mutters came from other men and women surrounding him. This wasn't an uncommon thing to see, in his opinion. Stagnation, he'd killed hundreds of these creatures. Sure, this one was big, but really not *that* big compared to half of the beasts he'd killed. For some reason, though, these people seemed to be astonished by it.

Landsmen.

Why did Aohd bring back the entire head? It was better to break them down at sea to conserve space in the holds.

"This is why I ain't never step'n onto a boat," one of the lads in front of him said. "Can you imagine having those teeth rip into ya?"

"These leviathan hunters are crazy!" another boy agreed.

Rowan harrumphed. Leviathans weren't dangerous. Sure, they could swallow a man whole, or rip an attack-boat into splinters, but they wouldn't bother a person if they didn't chase after them.

The derrick lowered the scaly head to the dock with a thump. Coagulated blood splattered on the planks in wet, green, gelatinous chunks. The smell was atrocious—sour melons and rotten meat. Rowan breathed in the foulness with fondness and let his memories take him back to some of his most favorite hunts.

"Careful, down there!" a man shouted. "It can't bite you, but the teeth can still sever the fingers from your hands if you ain't careful. And the spines can impale ya with one careless sneeze!"

CHAPTER
FOUR

owan looked up to see Aohd standing on the prow of his ship, a steadying hand grasping tightly to a stay line. His body swayed as the rope shifted under his weight. He was shirtless, a tuft of thin hair barely visible on a chest as thin and gangly as a slab of dried fish.

"We're not fools," one of the young men in front of Rowan called back to him.

"Not fools?" Aohd asked back, his voice tinted with confined mockery. "It don't take a fool to come afoul to these ruthless creatures, boy." Several members of the crowd turned to look at the young man, whose face turned red with embarrassment. "Unless you think the men that died fighting this creature were fools? Men who'd braved the kettle with its flesh melting waves of liquid fire? Men who never backed down when the beast, pierced by harpoons, splashed and slashed its razor-sharp fins in desperation?"

There was a slight lull in the man's speech as Rowan and apparently the rest of the crowd waited for Captain Aohd to ask yet another scorning question.

"No, sir," the boy replied, his shoulders creeping up higher to hide the shame.

"No," Aohd said, his voice low and contemplative. "The

sea do be filled with men. Brave men. None of them fools, I tell ya. None." By the time he spoke the last word, his voice was barely audible.

Then, with an obvious surge of energy, he spoke aloud once more. "The fools be here on the docks." He looked down his nose at them all, his eyes squinted as though he could hardly stand to see them. "Hiding behind boxes, barrels, and carts! Running from the winds instead of embracing them. Cowering from storms instead of challenging them from the rigg'n!" He was pointing a boney finger at them all now. "You all sicken me."

The folks that came to see the severed head scowled and started to move away in different directions. Rowan stayed where he stood. He understood Aohd completely. The tiny captain had been thinking of his fallen companions. Thinking of their bravery. How they risked their lives to swell an economy these landsmen enjoyed without ever having to risk it all. Watching men die was as traumatic as anything a person could endure. Rowan hoped he'd never have to knock on another widow's door to tell a teary-eyed woman her husband would never return to be with her again.

The sound of men's and women's voices faded as the crowd dispersed, angry at being judged unfairly. Rowan stood there alone with his thoughts. He still wasn't completely dry and a vibrant chill crept up his arms again. He should change into some dry clothes. Turning away from the severed leviathan head, Rowan rubbed his arms vigorously to bring back some warmth.

Lit torches cast flickering shadows on the docks as they illuminated busy workmen hustling about their tasks. The smell of fish was always strong here on the fisherman's wharf. Especially when passing a cart filled to bursting with Cuttertrout pulled from the dragger's nets.

What was it Aohd said about losing men? How many did

he lose? What happened out there? In the beginning, the man was agreeable, delighting in his tale, but when one ill-timed comment was spoken, the man turned completely and became quite hostile.

Rowan had seen this behavior before. Back when he was an understudy to Captain Culkin, one of his first hunts had gone horribly wrong and three attack boats had gone down and most of the men with them. Rowan had remained on the ship.

Almost thirty crewmen died that day and those that lived were never the same. Simply looking at a harpoon caused them to clam up, becoming unresponsive as they internally relived their memories of death.

They never sailed again.

Rowan was a greenhorn at the time with too little experience to know the men very well, or perhaps he, too, would have suffered the same. It was a stark reminder as to the dangerous nature of his profession. Seasoned and experienced fishermen barely had any business hunting leviathans.

He thought of his new cabin boy. Marek's lack of experience would certainly be a crutch. He'd need to moderate the boy's training. Bring him along slowly and not give him too much responsibility at first. *But I can't shelter the lad. He do be a sailor now, and a hunter.* Too much time on the sidelines could actually do more damage than instantly immersing him in combat.

Several dockworkers stopped Rowan on his short walk to the *Slayer*. "Captain Donchaad," said an eager young man pulling a bucket of lamp oil in a small cart. "How many dragons did you slay this time?" A few whiskers on his upper lip glowed translucent in the surrounding torchlight.

"Rowan, lad," an ancient sailor asked, holding out a withered hand to stop him. "Would ya be will'n to take an old fisherman with ya on yer next voyage? Can't stand the thought of die'n on solid ground, ya see?"

Rowan had no time for either of these conversations and brushed them off with a short explanation and a sincere smile. He understood the old man's desire, but he wasn't really all that ready to embrace death just yet.

He reached the gangplank and darted onto his ship. Home at last. The deck beneath him swayed ever-so-gently. He let out a sigh of relief. These islands with their stable roads and buildings that never moved was a tad unnerving.

The ship was silent save for shouting workers down on the docks.

Most of the crew were gone, enjoying themselves at Mickey's or one of the bars and clubs in the *Flats*. Stagnation, some of them could have been at the Comsos for all he knew.

They'd soon come back, though. Rowan had a standing order for each employee to return to the ship every morning with Belinus' appearance over the eastern horizon. When that sun rose, the men would appear and they would make their departure.

He hastened to the bridge, opening the door to his cabin. Shadows covered most everything in darkness, though some moonlight shone through the aft windows providing just enough illumination for Rowan to see without needing to fire up a lamp. He sat down at the table with an exhausted sigh and elevated his feet, relieving the ache he hadn't realized was there.

Abandinus preserve me. I can't wait to raise anchor and get off this damn island. Back to the sea where I can hunt in peace.

Rowan let out a sigh, cupped the back of his head in calloused hands, and stared at the ceiling. Faint creaks of shifting timber echoed in the stillness. Infant waves slapped curiously at the side of the hull. Aohd's behavior unnerved him more than Cass's. What *had* happened on that hunt? He pushed the thought away and leaned forward, fingering the hardware on the front of the table.

The drawer under the table screeched as Rowan slid it open. He gathered up all the documents and torn segments of maps and put them on the tabletop. He added some bits of brown wax, an iron stamp with his personal seal, and a few spare wicks to the pile before wedging the hooked end of a steel quill in a small gap at the corner of the drawer base. He pulled upward to reveal a hidden compartment.

Delicately he lifted out a pair of struck-glass earrings and laid them on his palm. A glimmer of emerald light reflected moon rays in tiny, bright laces of pale green.

They were Birgitta's.

Rowan loved tagging along with her through wide-open beaches and high sandy peaks as she searched for lightning struck glass. Whenever she found some, Rowan would take it to Dun' Armagh, one of the two neighboring kingdoms, to have the finest silversmiths in the world cast jewelry for Birgitta to display them in.

These were her favorite.

These and the sapphire pendant Rowan faithfully wore around his neck, were all he allowed himself to keep with him in memory of his wife. The rest of her things were all back at the manor. Exactly where she'd kept them before her...

Before she...

Before...

ROWAN WOKE TO THE SOUND OF THE WIND SHRILLING THROUGH the stays and masts two levels above him like a flock of long-tailed Jaegers whistling through the air. Restless, he rubbed sleep from his eyes. What was a little wind?

It was dark, there in the cabin he shared with his wife. Birgitta was sound asleep. Rowan could feel her pressed familiarly against him. She was warm, almost too warm, being seven months pregnant. He pulled off the thin linen sheet to let the night air cool his body. What time was it? He hoped there was still enough darkness to get a few more hours of sleep.

He wasn't looking forward to the next day's activities, not exactly, if he were truthful with himself. But he'd do it for Birgitta who feared the nightmares of her unborn baby were actually premonitions of things to come.

Rowan was a seaman. He loved the wind and the waves, the heaving sea and the screaming gulls. He was also ridiculously super-stitious and agreed whole-heartedly that they should make the month-long journey to this distant continent, west of his island home.

So they sailed to Dun' Armagh—a flat, grassy land he and Birgitta would visit to ride horses through a countryside that glistened yellow-gold in the light of Belinus and Belinos' rays—to see the Obeah, a witch doctor with strange powers that unnerved him to his core.

That's why they were in this confined cabin. The ship they were on had already dropped anchor in the bay late last night. Most folks had asked a crewman to row them ashore so they could stay in one of the fancy inns on the beach, but Birgitta had obliged him and allowed them to stay the night on the ship where he felt most comfortable.

He was a lucky man and he knew it.

He rubbed his eyes, and blinked them to life. It wasn't just dark, he realized. It was black. He listened again to the wind, his hackles rising by the second. The hair on the nape of his neck seemed to lift him clean out of bed. Everything felt alive around him. The walls and floors creaked and moaned like the inhabitants of a hospital's sickroom. He wished he could see—see anything at all—but the dark-ness suffocated his vision.

Rowan sat up quickly, thinking to poke his head out the door. Maybe there was enough light out there to see what was going on. He nearly lost his balance. Flinging out a hand, he braced himself on the bedrail to keep from actually falling onto the floor. One of the chests they'd brought suddenly shifted from its position, screeching loudly as it began moving across the floor on its own.

Abandinus preserve us!

A gaping pit opened in Rowan's stomach and he instantly broke out in tiny beads of ice-cold sweat. He knew right then exactly what was happening. If they were to survive this night, they'd have to move, and move fast.

"Birgitta!" He had to scream over the noise. How hadn't he realized how loud it was before now? "Birgitta!" he shouted again. Light suddenly filled the room in a sharp flash of gold and Rowan could finally see. His entire cabin was listing to the starboard at an angle no sailor hoped to experience. "Darling, wake up! Birgitta!" He shook her, none-too-gently, to get her to wake.

Another flash of light—lightning, it had to be. The storm outside was worse than he could have imagined. This ship was going down.

In that light of flashing fire, Birgitta opened her eyes.

Green eyes.

Pale, emerald, terrified eyes.

RAPID KNOCKS FELL ON THE DOOR. ROWAN FLINCHED, THE memory fading in an instant, and nearly dropped the earrings. He gasped, sucking sweet, life-sustaining, air into his body. Why had he stopped breathing? He set the jewelry down on the table, half expecting them to slide off on their own. He reminded himself he was no longer in that memory. There was no storm. There was no oncoming tragedy.

With a racing heart, he called out, "Come!"

The door opened to admit Aifric and a short, skinny lad standing half concealed behind him. "I beg yer pardon, Captain," Aifric said, stepping inside the room. "I've come to fetch miss Asy's... uh... gift?" Aifric's eyes fell to the desk where the earrings lay. The man had good vision to spot them so easily in the dim light.

"Yes, of course," Rowan said, taking a clean handkerchief from his pocket and wrapping up the earrings. He stood, half expecting to fall forward. Again, he had to remind himself he was no longer in that memory. He shook his head slightly, not wanting Aifric to see his discomfort.

Rowan walked around the desk and handed the folded cloth to his first mate. "Is this the boy?" Rowan asked, whipping the lad's hat off his head to get a look at him. He had thick red hair a bit darker than most with hair the same color, and more freckles than he could count. The boy's gaze never shifted away from Rowan's. He liked that. "Marek, is it?"

"Aye, Captain," Aifric said, stepping aside to let Rowan get a full view of the new cabin boy. "My oldest nephew, he do be. His mother is my second oldest and only surviving sister. He's got a younger brother, Quinn, just shedd'n the diaper as we speak. A good time for him to be get'n out and joining yer crew, I think."

Rowan leaned forward, leveling his eyes with Marek's. "Is this yer first time on a ship Marek?" he asked.

"No, sir," Marek said, squaring his shoulders. Rowan looked up at Aifric who smiled. Hadn't the man told him his nephew had never been on a sailing vessel?

"Ever sailed before?" Rowan asked, switching up his question. The lad darted a look up at his uncle before hesitantly shaking his head. "But ye do be a fast learner, don't ya?" he asked, guiding the boy's eyes back to him.

"Aye," Marek said with a small smile.

"And yer eager to kill leviathans?"

"Aye." Marek's smile grew a little wider and his answer was a smidge louder.

"And I'll bet yer eager to start mak'n some gold too?" he said, standing straight.

"Aye, sir," he said with a slight laugh.

"Well, lad," Rowan said, standing tall and cramming the boy's hat back on his head. "This I can promise ya. Work harder than you've ever worked in yer life. Listen more carefully than ya've ever listened. Learn everything ya can 'bout runn'n a ship and doing yer part. Do this and I promise ya you'll make more gold than ya've ever imagined and you'll kill more leviathans than anyone will ever believe. How's that sound'n to ya, lad?"

The boy laughed. "Sounds great, Captain."

"Show the boy his hammock and trunk, Aifric, an' take that," he gestured to the parcel containing the earrings, "on up to Breanna." Rowan walked over to his trundle bed and sat down on the soft linen sheets. When Aifric nodded his acquiescence and shut the door behind him, Rowan collapsed onto his pillow, exhausted. He half expected to feel the bed tilt and dump him onto the floor, but he reminded himself he was no longer in that—*aagh!*

He hated those damn memories. They snuck up on him without warning. The memories were always worse when he was drunk. But he wasn't really all that drunk now, and when he was, his thoughts had been more on his daughter. He hoped those earrings would... What? Remind her of her mother? Her father?

She had no memories of either of them. He didn't even know if she was even able to retain memory.

He closed his eyes and banished thoughts of his daughter from his mind. In fact, he tried to banish *all* thoughts from his mind. But green flashes kept streaking across his closed lids.

Green flashes and memories of Birgitta.

PART THREE

The sea is a masterpiece of Abandinus's creation. A watery vault of untold and undiscovered riches, open to those brave enough to plunder its bounty. A hidden world, blind to the cares of those who live above its surf. In the extreme of its unfathomable beauty and siren magnetism, its insouciance for human life makes fools of us all.

—Fergus Culkin, captain of the Domnall, *leviathan ship of the first class, personal ship of the king*

CHAPTER
FIVE

Rowan sat alone in his cabin aboard his ship, the *Slayer of the Sea*. A warm bottle of Bushmill's whiskey rested precariously against his half-unbuttoned, sweat-soaked linen shirt. The liquor inside the bottle tipped gently from side to side as he struggled to fight the torpor.

The cabin was silent save for the rhythmic rumble of the captain's breath. His head propped against the rest of a high-backed chair that shifted in concert with the imprisoned whiskey, while the heels of his bare feet lay atop the table holding his maps and compass. Rowan balanced on the pinnacle of slumber, his fear of sleeping through the kettle—a leviathan breaching the surface—anchored him to near wakefulness.

It wasn't like the captain to be idle during the light of day, but the uncommon lack of activity in these waters beyond the atolls of Manks had Rowan longing for the adventure only dreams could provide in this barren part of the sea. That and there was nothing to do. Their daily drills had already been completed as well as the upkeep on weathered sails and rigging.

It's been months since we left port and still no damn leviathans.

Not even a single steam cloud. We'll run out of food before we even half-fill the holds.

Groaning more from frustration than fatigue, Rowan stood, nearly losing the bottle as he got to his feet. He walked unsteadily to the open door leading to the bridge. Weathered wooden stairs descended onto a deck that seemed almost lifeless, aside from a few men swabbing the planks that made up both decks. Letting the deck planks dry out shrunk the wood, creating gaps between the slats that could potentially let water flood into the vessel.

The men not slapping wet mops on the deck sat in whatever shade they could find, though the positions of Belinus and Belenos high above left little to offer them by way of a cool repose. When both suns were up, even the smallest tasks tended to get quite miserable.

Rowan refused to let the men belowdecks in the afternoon unless they were sharpening knives, gaffs, or harpoons. Stagnation take him if they were ever unprepared when a leviathan breached the tropic skin of the open sea.

Leviathans were uncanny and unpredictable. It was Rowan's passion to slay as many of the heartless beasts as he could thrust a spear into, though their iron-like scales and coral-tough hide made it difficult for the men aboard the *Slayer* to penetrate flesh.

Difficult, but not impossible.

To say he loved this chosen profession would be a mockery to how intense and deeply his feeling truly dove. It consumed him like a whirling typhoon hungrily ripping hovels from the windward side of an island, and pervaded every corner of his brain like rainwater filling the hull of a floundering felucca.

Rowan returned to his seat and lifted the bottle to his lips. He had to be careful not to get too drunk. He knew a captain working on a Privileged vessel that liked the bottle a little too much and the crew mutinied on him, throwing him into the sea without a trial. Rowan laughed contemplatively, thinking of those ships. Like pirates, they were, only licensed by the king to rob his citizens blind.

One advantage of an empty hold, he laughed sarcastically to himself, *I can send those Privileged bastards on their way without an ounce of gold to add to their coffers.*

"Ere she boils, lads! Ere she boils!"

Rowan's heart froze for just an instant before he came alert. *Demons below! We found one!* He flew to his feet, the heavy, brown bottle of Bushmill's crashing to the wood floor with a resounding thud. Whiskey gurgled from confinement, soaking into the deck boards, but not before Rowan was lifting a different bottle to his lips. He coughed and sputtered, warm vinegar spraying across the room, though he held down as much as he could. *Stagnation, I better not be too drunk for this!*

He stumbled out the door seconds later, his shouts trailing as the unfettered animal inside him was unleashed, eager for confrontation.

"Where is he, Aifric?" Rowan shouted, though the man was only feet from him tending the wheel. He quickly scanned the water surrounding them for the steam cloud, but saw nothing other than calm, flat, ocean. He looked upward at the gull's nest. Rich, blue, cloudless sky silhouetted the man perched high above the main mast. Not much of him showed over the rim of the basket, but he could see the man's brass looking-glass pointing out over the ocean like a godly finger giving direction from on high.

"Port side, Captain!" the first mate replied, over the shouts from the bustling men on deck. Spinning the wheel counter clockwise he said, "You can barely make out the plume if you look close. Stagnation take us, if this were a cloudy day there'd be no telling if Jannon could'a spotted it. As it is, the man has eyes like a hawk."

"Bring us around," he urged Aifric. "These blasted monsters can move, and I ain't will'n to let 'em get away from us. Not after all this time." He ran to the ladder attached to the outer wall of his cabin and scrambled onto the upper deck. It was the highest part of the ship, not counting the three masts with their white, semi-slack sails.

"I'm turn'n as fast as I can, Captain, but the wind ain't will'n." Aifric faced the nearly non-existent wind and shook his fist. "Blow, damn ya, blow!"

Rowan scowled, wondering if more sail were needed to catch what little wind they had. The slightest gust could make all the difference.

He looked across the water to see a small speck of white on the distant horizon. Sure enough, he could see the kettle. Steam rose into the air like a barely visible, outcast cloud sitting sadly on the ocean surface.

"Stagnation, it's too far out! Aifric, get those blasted sails up on both starboard and port hulls," Rowan cried. Excitement began to slip away, doubt and unease forcing its way in. With their quarry so far out, overtaking it just might be impossible. "Starboard sail first, Aifric. We need to get the proper bearing before raising the port mast."

"Aye, Captain," the man responded, holding the wheel in place. He relayed the order to the deck boss below. "Berit!" he shouted. "Get that starboard sail up!" The middle-aged man waved his understanding before shouting to the men around him.

Rowan watched as eight crewmen ran to the starboard rail, scrambling like insects over the thirty-foot bridge to the parallel hull where canvas flaps were untied and flung aside to dangle over the edge.

Abandinus grace us, this be a triple-hulled ship. May its shallow draft carry us ever faster over the water! No ship ever built, comparable in size to the *Slayer of the Sea,* could match her in speed. Beneath the canvas, a heavy mast thick as a man's thigh lay parallel to the hull. The larger end was secured to a steel brace by a heavy metal dowel allowing the mast to pivot as it was raised.

Berit's voice rose over the shouting men as he ordered the crew to raise the mast. "Grab the lines, lads. The wenches be wait'n back at port! Show 'em how tall you can get it!" While several men grabbed the hoist lines, ready to pull, three others ran to the aft end and grabbed the top of the mast. "Heave, damn you, heave!" Berit shouted encouragingly. While those three men lifted, five others pulled the lines attached to pulleys at the bow that coursed back to the center of the mast, and slowly the cylindrical beam began to rise.

"Atta boy, lads! Keep pull'n, damn your hides," Berit pressed. The men grunted as they heaved hard on the lines, sounding like a hull full of men staggering out of their hammocks after a long night of drink.

Rowan's thoughts drifted back to the bottle of Bushmill's he'd left on the floor of his cabin. He should have finished off the dregs before leaving. *Not now, boil my hide. I can drink in celebration if we can conquer this beast,* he thought eagerly.

Below him on the starboard hull, the men finished raising the mast. Kier, the greenhorn, climbed the twenty-foot pole, a canvas sail tucked into the back of his trousers. He stopped well short of the top and Rowan thought the man might be too low to attach the lateen canvas sail, but Kier's long arms reached just far enough to engage the clasp before the green-horn slid down the beam to land on the hull with a reverberating thud.

Stagnation, that hull's emptier than an oarsman's belly nine months at sea, he thought. *I better make more gold than this to keep the men fed and my sister-in-law happy enough to continue taking care of my child.* Old Leary was a fine cook, but when the galley was empty, all they could do was starve their way back to port.

In seconds the starboard hull was in full sail and he could feel the boat turning faster. "Well done, lads!" Rowan shouted down to his men. They looked up to him, and he could plainly see their smiles. The greenhorn's face was flush, no doubt excited to have his captain's favor. They ran across the deck and onto the bridge leading to the port hull, where they labored to raise the other mast and hang a sail.

"Now we can fly, Captain!" Aifric called up to him. "Bearing dead ahead. We'll be on it faster than ya can spend the gold we make kill'n it!"

Rowan skipped half the ladder altogether and jumped, landing deftly on the bridge. "You just keep us on the current bearing, mate," he said clapping a strong hand over Aifric's shoulder, "lest Jannon tells ya otherwise. I got the rest of it from here."

"Aye, Captain."

Smiling at his first mate, he ran to the stairs and—skipping every other step—landed on the deck, eager to make final preparations for the kettle.

This do be the hardest part of all, catch'n up to her before she goes cold. Rowan could never tolerate a leviathan diving back down to deeper waters.

They were too far away to launch the attack boats just yet. The men would be exhausted and unable to fight by the time they got there. He was left with one choice. Let the ship do her job and sail them closer, even if he did feel like a snail on the water. Rowan paced the bridge anxiously while the slow movement of the ship taxed his patience every bit as ruthlessly as any crooked Privileged captain.

Abandinus, please help us find more wind.

CHAPTER
SIX

A top a coil of line resting on the deck near the main mast, Marek picked at a loose strand of fiber while all around him the ship was in turmoil. Men ran in every direction, their voices loud and sharp, as they called to one another.

"Stand by the Spanker!"

"Let go clew lines and sheet ho!"

"Strike topgallants. Let fly sheets!"

"There's a snarl in the gasket!"

Little of it made any sense to Marek. Despite his limited knowledge, anxiety ate at his insides as he thought of all the ways he could be useful, but the captain's orders were the captain's orders. "Keep out of the way, my boy," he'd said. "This be man's work, not a child's. I'll call ya when I need ya, not beforehand."

Becoming a man was what Marek wanted more than anything. Being told to keep out of the way did nothing to fill the void left behind when his father had up and disappeared, leaving him and his baby brother Quinn fatherless. *That was what, four years ago now? I can barely remember him, that bastard. I'll show Quinn what a man* should *be.*

"Ready the attack boats, Berit!" he heard the captain call.

The man practically flew down the steps from the bridge. "I'll need them to launch at a moment's notice."

"Right, Captain!" replied a voice from behind Marek. He turned and saw the deck boss—rigid and stern with eyes that glowered like a disapproving parent. Berit grabbed a tall, wiry man by the collar who just happened to be passing by with an armful of harpoons, their steel tips glinting crisp in the bright noon suns.

"Finnian!" Berit roared, "Enough with the harpoons, man, double check the tack! I don't wanna find myself deep in the Kettle short on line." He shoved the man as if to help him on his way, and several harpoons slipped to the deck. Marek jumped off his coil of line to help retrieve the fallen weapons, but got a hateful scowl from the deck boss. He scrambled back atop the coil, put his chin in his hands, and watched Finnian clumsily gather up the harpoons. *I could have helped. Uncle Aifric wouldn't have convinced the captain to take me on if he thought I was useless.*

Berit was a veteran aboard these types of ships, Marek reminded himself. The man boasted often of the fifteen years he'd hunted with Captain Donchaad, as well as the twenty years he'd spent working on other ships before that. Marek didn't much like the blustery old man, but he respected his knowledge.

"This is the last of it, boss," Finnian replied, displaying the now full armload of weaponry. Though he was the cook's assistant, he sure knew his way around a leviathan ship. Marek had never seen him wander the decks like most of the younger crewmen. Every move he made was done with calculation and purpose.

"It better be," Berit said. "Captain wants the boats ready to go. And remember to double-check everything." Marek wondered why Finnian needed to double-check anything when they had gone through all their drills a couple hours ago. Everything should already be ready to go.

"Aye, sir!" replied Finnian.

It was Aifric, Marek's uncle, who Marek looked up to most. The first mate reminded him of his father, the same strong face, the same pale blue eyes, but for all the similarities, he was completely different in temperament and stature. Aifric was a hard-built man, not too tall, with a smattering of grey decorating his blonde temples. He was calm and gentle and could snap someone in half with the slightest provocation.

At times Marek wondered what it would have been like to have Aifric as his father. His first day aboard the *Slayer of the Sea*, Aifric took Marek under his wing. If he was ever unsure of what was expected of him, Aifric was always willing to give him some pointers. The man's advice had kept him out of the kettle on more than one occasion.

"Hey, cabin boy!" Marek looked up to see Berit scowling down on him.

"Sir?" he asked, getting to his feet.

"Get down to the galley, quick as ya can. Old Leary's got bait fer ya," he said, shooing him off with a wave of his hands. "Go, before I pickle yer oysters and feed 'em to the sharks. Go!" Marek didn't waste a stutter. *Finally, something to do!* He ran from his position under the main mast and headed to the companion ladder under the bridge that went down to the hold. He bolted down the steps, counting all eleven of them as he went and made his way past the bunks and hammocks to the forecastle.

The galley was mostly dark, though some light did stream in through a cracked open hatch leading to the deck above. A cross-patterned brace fit over the opening to keep the crew from falling in on accident. The stove, he noticed with a scowl, was old and rusty, or maybe that was spilled slop. It looked as though it hadn't been cleaned in ages. The room smelled of charred coal and birchwood.

Oak barrels were stacked high in the corners with the names of their contents stenciled on the sides. Beans, salted pork, and even more beans. A few square crates of vegetables filled the empty places around the room, leaving very little space for walking around. The vegetables were most likely rotten. The cook hadn't fed them *any* in the entire month they'd been at sea. *I better not get scurvy.*

"Leary, sir?" he said, spying the old man sitting on a three-legged chair, snoring away. Marek stepped closer. "Leary!" The old man snorted when Marek gave him a firm shake, and he came awake, arms swinging in surprise. Marek was ready for it and stepped backward to avoid the flailing spoon that came within an inch of his nose.

"What is it? What's going on?" Old Leary rubbed his eyes with the heels of his hands and gave his head a quick shake. "Marek?" he said, recognizing him. "What's the meaning of this? I was dead asleep, something an old man like me needs more than an eight-year-old whelp like yourself."

"Eleven, sir," he said, grinning in wry amusement as he remembered the number of steps leading down from the deck.

"Eleven what, lad?"

"I'm eleven years old. Not eight, sir."

"Whatever floats your hull, son. Why are you down here anyway? I'm sorry, but I won't have nuth'n edible for hours yet. You'll have to wait your turn like ever'body else." He folded his arms and closed his eyes looking as though he were about to go back to sleep. Marek couldn't let that happen.

"Jannon's spotted a leviathan, sir, and Captain Donchaad has us turned and headed straight for it. We'll be there in minutes!"

"What? Leviathan? Well why didn't you say so earlier?"

The old man lunged out of his chair and hurried over to where a particularly filthy pair of barrels sat near the door. Marek had passed by them when he entered the room, not really noticing them. They were larger than the other barrels, with lids that fit inside like a cork in a bottle.

"If I don't get you back up there in time with me bait, the captain'll have me head. Now get over here." The cook grabbed a basket of vegetables and emptied them onto the floor.

Marek pursed his mouth at the mistreatment of food, even if it was almost inedible. Without a working father, his mother had to scrape for whatever scraps she could feed them.

Using a long bar of steel, Old Leary wedged open one of the barrels. A distinct hiss resonated from the sealed lid as it opened. A putrid stench followed on invisible heels to fill the room with the most malodorous scent Marek had ever smelled. His stomach boiled and his mouth started sweating.

"Me own secret recipe, lad," Old Leary said, putting down the metal bar and grabbing a pair of extremely long tongs. He had to use both hands when he dipped them into the muck that bubbled and glurped. "Learnt it from me grandfather, I did. He worked for the Domnall family before old Marcas went and became king. His father before him was one of the finest leviathan hunters to sail the sea and me own grandfather cooked up the same recipe for bait as what you see here." Wincing with strain, he lifted a large chunk of disgusting meat from the barrel, the foul marinade dripping from it in green sheets of slimy filth.

"Is that leviathan meat?" Marek asked.

"Aye, lad," he replied with a wink. "The foulest thing a man can get his hands on."

Catching a particularly nasty whiff of the spoiled meat, Marek's stomach heaved. *How can he talk so much? If I don't hold my breath, I'll... I'll...* He didn't want to finish that thought for fear of it actually happening.

"Luckily, we won't ever have to eat the stuff," Old Leary said with a scowl. He probably had to eat some once. "Starving to death would be a better end to your misery if you were ever unfortunate enough to be in such a pickle."

"*Cabin boy!*" a voice bellowed from above deck, followed by the stomp of an angry foot.

"Stagnation, it's Berit!" Marek said, suddenly eager to get moving. What Berit would do to him if he dallied... Marek didn't want to find out. "Leary, please hurry. I have to go!"

The cook placed the head-sized chunk of leviathan meat in the basket, followed by a second. It hit the bottom with a sickening slap that almost jarred the whole basket out of Marek's hands. Stagnation it was heavy.

"Off with ya, lad!" Old Leary shouted, though it was just the two of them in the small room. "Hope ya don't lose yer head fer dawdl'n too long!" Marek barely heard him. The sooner he delivered his putrid parcel to the deck boss the better. Hopefully his stomach would hold out long enough. He reached the deck a moment later.

"What under the suns took ye so long?" Berit scolded, once Marek made it topside. "Any idiot with a brain could'a done a better job of it. Your mother should'a tossed ye overboard as a bab as soon as kept ye. Hand it over." He yanked the basket out of Marek's hands and threw it atop his shoulder, not even wincing from the stench. The man was harder than Marek expected. Marinade oozed through the basket onto Berit's shirt. Marek didn't want to stick around when the deck boss found out.

Marek ran across the deck back to the main mast, his preferred area for observing the goings on. Excited to have been useful, even though his task came grudgingly from a man he disliked, he became more keenly aware of the activity around him. Under the port bridge, the attack boats were being lowered. A pulley system and a bridle, tied bow to stern, secured them where they could be kept out of the way.

From what Uncle Aifric told him, no third-class leviathan ship the size of the *Slayer of the Sea* had double catamaran's like theirs. The starboard and port hulls, he'd said, were primarily for storing goods. There was also something about making the ship go faster, but he couldn't quite remember the details.

"Marek, lad! Where ya be, my boy?" It was the captain.

"Over here, sir," he shouted, looking around not really knowing from where the captain had hailed him.

"Can ye get me suit, Marek?" he heard the captain shout again. Marek felt a hand on his shoulder and jumped. He turned to see Captain Donchaad standing over him. "I need me suit, lad. It'll get hot out there in the kettle, and if he's a monstrous rogue, he'll have me for soup without it."

"Aye, Captain. You bet, I can," he said with confidence.

"Wonderful," the captain said with a smile. "Bring it to the starboard attack boat as quickly as possible." The powerful man turned and walked toward the boat he'd indicated. "Do it fast," he shouted after him, "and I'll let ya tag along!"

CHAPTER
SEVEN

Dread, following on the boot heels of excitement, filled Marek as he realized he had no idea what 'suit' the captain was referring to. He knew it was a leviathan suit, but he'd never seen it before and didn't know where exactly to find it.

Uncle Aifric will know!

Climbing the companion ladder to the bridge, he found Aifric manning the wheel.

"Have ya seen Leary, lad?" his uncle inquired before Marek could ask his question. "The old codger's supposed to take the wheel for me so I can join the hunt!"

"Uh, no, sir," Marek replied, his hands beginning to feel sweaty. "But I'm supposed to get the captain his suit?"

"In his cabin, Cabin Boy. The drawer under his bed." Aifric thumbed toward the solid door behind him.

With a smile, and an eager sense of excitement, Marek darted into Captain Donchaad's cabin.

It was a large room, sparsely furnished with wood paneled walls and floors. Marek stared in awe. This was the first time he'd passed through that doorway. The room was, and wasn't, what he'd expected. Two chairs and a small, cluttered desk sat in the middle of the chamber. A sextant and a magnetic compass held loose charts and maps in place. However, in high winds and increased swells, nothing would hold that table down. It was simply too small and light.

Ten or fifteen chests lined the walls. What they held, Marek had no idea. But he noticed a strip of wood nailed to the floor with a lip facing the chests. An undercut, he realized. Each chest had a small ledge extending outward on the bottom that fit under the strip of wood to keep them from sliding around in bad weather. The genius of the captain never ceased to amaze him.

Marek turned his attention to the bed box nestled snugly against the port bulkhead. A flat, barely recognizable pillow lay atop a lumpy, sweat-stained mattress. A yellowed linen blanket sat rumpled on the floor at the foot of the bed. The captain probably hasn't used that blanket in months. Not in this heat. Marek wiped a few beads of sweat that had gathered since he entered the stuffy room.

The bed sat about a foot and a half off the floor, and Marek noticed a slit cut into the bed's facing. It looked wide enough to get in a few fingers. He pulled on the facing and it began to creak as it slid outward.

As Marek pulled it out further, his jaw nearly hit the floor with astonishment. From end to end lay the most magnificent suit he'd ever seen. It was constructed from what looked like leather, but it shimmered almost metallic in the sunlight that streamed from the aft windows. *Dragonhide!* Marek had never seen such a magnificent dragonhide suit up close before, but he'd heard all about them from stories told by the great leviathan hunters of the sea.

He marveled at the suit. It was all of one piece and littered with copper buckles where the garment opened to allow a man to step inside. As he crouched down to touch it, the leather felt smooth and supple, save for the stiff plates of stone wood armor sewn into the material. What would it be like to wear it?

"Marek!" He was shaken from his reverie by Aifric's familiar voice. He was silhouetted in the doorway. "Better make it quick, Cabin Boy. Old Leary's just replaced me. We'll be shoving off in seconds."

Aifric didn't stay to see if Marek heard his warning. The man was there one moment and gone the next. Marek didn't wait either. He scooped the suit into his arms. *Stagnation, it's almost as light as linen.* He darted from the cabin, leaving the drawer slid out and empty. Portly Leary whooped after him as Marek stumbled down the steps.

"I got it here, sir," Marek said, standing on the starboard bridge, the attack boat floating—yet still tied securely—below him. It was filled with men settling oars into oarlocks.

"Took ya long enough, lad," the captain said, smiling up at him from the bow of the attack boat. Marek was getting tired of hearing that. "But I thank ya, nonetheless." Satisfied with the words of gratitude, Marek sat on the bridge and readied himself to slide down into the boat.

"Not this one, lad. We're full up," the captain said, stowing his suit in a hatch under the bow. "I'd like ya to tag along in the other boat."

How under the suns did the captain know he was climbing down? He wasn't even looking at him.

"Go, cabin boy," the captain said when Marek didn't move right away. "Get a move on." A few chuckles followed the admonition. He didn't see who'd jeered, and didn't really care. He just knew he had to cross the deck to the port bridge as fast as he could.

It didn't take him long to get there.

"Aifric!" he shouted, running up the port catamaran. "Wait! Captain said I was coming with you."

"Then jump in, lad, on the double. We're already shove'n off."

"Aye sir," he said.

It was Desmond, a short, portly man of about thirty, who reached up and helped him slide down into the boat. "There's an empty seat up by the first mate. Go on, now."

Marek high-stepped past the men and over the seats that ran perpendicular to the centerline of the boat. He had to make his way carefully past coils of line and giant metal hooks with wooden handles to the empty seat next to Aifric.

"Unclip the bridle, boys," the stout man shouted. "We're off!"

A chorus of loud cheers went up from the men around him, their voices raucous and filled with excitement.

There were six oarlocks on each side of the attack boat with a sailor manning each one. The first mate sat at the prow calling out directions. With the first simultaneous pull of the oars, the boat shot forward. Marek was not prepared for it. He fell backward off his seat, knowing his head was about to connect with the bench behind him, but something stopped Marek's fall. He opened his eyes and looked up. A smiling Aifric held fast to the front of his linen shirt.

"You bloody that head of yours and the captain'll be want'n to use ya as bait, he will. Not only that, but yer moth-er'd have me hide if I brought you back broken." Aifric said it with a smile that made Marek feel easy about his warning. As the man pulled him back up, he laughed and gave him a solid slap on the back. It nearly knocked the breath out of him. "Keep ahold of your seat and anticipate each pull. You'll get used to it, lad. Who knows, you could be manning an oar yourself soon."

Marek hoped not. Just getting the boat in the water had apparently been a tougher job than he realized. The men were already dripping with sweat.

When they came up on the bow of the ship, Marek saw the other boat well ahead of them—about three boat-lengths away.

"Heave to," the first mate called. "Can't let the captain get too far of a lead. Now heave!" The men rowed and grunted in unison, their oars dipping into the water and propelling them forward.

Marek looked ahead to the captain's boat. *They're not that far ahead of us. They're just—*

Then he spied the kettle.

White clouds billowed up before them like a monolithic gout of steam. He swallowed nervously. It was still a ways out, but already it looked ominous, and the boats were making excellent time. Marek estimated they'd be on the kettle in three or four minutes.

"Store the oars, gents." Aifric shouted. "Time to get your gear on."

Marek was confused. What gear? The thuds and scrapes of oars being pulled in and set aside made him turn to see what the men were about. They each stood and lifted their vacated seats. The benches opened on hinges and they were reaching inside for—*suits!* Dragonhide suits just like the captain's.

The men stripped down to cut-off linen trousers, the ends frayed at the knee. He laughed inside, looking at the older Desmond and Finnian in particular. Their skin was paler than the billowing steam cloud. His amusement was cut short as a shimmering suit was thrown over his head.

"Stop yer grinn'n and put this on," Connal said. He was a no-nonsense fellow, no doubt made that way by his bright red hair the color of a superstitious sunrise.

Lifting the dragonhide suit off his head Marek felt a growing excitement build in his stomach. He quickly stripped down and grabbed the buckles on the front of the suit, opening it so he could step inside.

"Turn it around, lad." He looked up and saw Aifric, his own suit fit firmly over his body, though the hood hung down his back. It was tight, but the man looked to be in no discomfort. He crouched down to help him. "You gotta turn it around, see? You step in like that, and the buckles will be on your back. You want them on your front so you can tighten 'em yerself." Once Aifric said it, it made perfect sense. It would have taken Marek a few times trying on his own to get it right otherwise.

As he fastened the buckles, the oarsmen resumed their rowing.

This time he actually fell. The men laughed uproariously, and Marek blushed, his cheeks and ears hot with blood. But he felt no pain from the fall, though he knew he'd hit his elbow hard on his seat. Did the suit stop him from getting hurt? *Stagnation, this is incredible.*

He quickly scrambled to his feet, ready for the next pull, and reclaimed his spot next to his uncle. The thin, shimmering leather flexed like his own skin. Other than the pressure of the snug fit, he barely felt it. Looking at his arms and legs, he thought he could make out the thin hairs pressed against his skin. *It's nearly transparent,* he thought with wonder. *Does all dragonhide do this?* But he didn't ask it aloud, for when he looked up, he nearly choked on the unasked question.

The kettle.

It was only a few boat-lengths ahead of them, like a pillar of wet, white fire.

Bubbles of air burst as they broke the surface of the water. Hundreds of bubbles—hundreds of thousands of bubbles— boiled like a writhing school of herring threatened by yellow-finned predators, emitting streams of steam that coalesced to produce the massive cloud that loomed high above them. The noise it made was distinct, like the echo of a thousand kernels of rahn popping in a cast-iron pan.

The captain's boat was on the opposite side of the kettle, barely visible through the torrent of scorching hot water and steam. Each man aboard shimmered in the haze like specters escaping from the underworld, rowing with all their might.

"Whatever ya do, lad," came Connal's stern voice behind him, "don't fall in the water." He paused to pull his oar, grunting with the effort. "That suit'll protect ya from getting your skin melted off, but it won't stop *all* the heat. It'll burn as though you've been in the suns fer hours." He heaved again. "Nor will it stop the leviathan from make'n lunch out'a ya."

The leviathan.

Stagnation! With all the steam and bubbles, he'd forgot about the leviathan!

PART
FOUR

It's a sorrowful fact of sea life, the similarity between leviathan and man. Both can smell the delicious stench of gold with its enticing call to take what you can, and neither one can resist its magnetic pull. However, I've seen more men killed by a captain's selfish, desperate greed than by a leviathan's wrenching, tearing teeth.

—Fergus Culkin, captain of the Domnall, *leviathan ship of the first class, personal ship of the king*

CHAPTER
EIGHT

None of the stories Marek had heard from the dockworkers gave this moment the grandeur and anxiety it deserved. It was almost crippling. The heat coming off the water nearly suffocated him, and sweat coated the inside of his suit making his skin unnaturally slick. A shiver ran through him.

The heel of Marek's foot tapped rhythmically on the wooden planks beneath. For the moment, he had nothing to do but watch. The oarsmen had their rowing, but Marek had nothing to occupy his time except for a nervous energy he was unable to channel.

They were skimming across the shimmering sea. The bow of the attack boat cut through the water like a fillet knife through cutter-trout. As they came abreast of the kettle with its blistering, boiling bubbles, Marek looked down, squinting to see beneath the turmoil.

Through the steam and water Marek saw something that stilled his breath and nearly stopped his heart. The outline of an enormous shadow, blacker than a starless night sky, swam methodically beneath him. It seemed to pull the excitement and confidence from his soul to fill it with the darkest memories of his life.

Now and then he caught a slight shimmer of yellow down in the blackness.

At five attack boats in comparison, maybe even six, it dwarfed all the imaginings of his childhood. *Stagnation, it might even be bigger than the ship!* He couldn't be certain of its length. Things in the water never looked their actual size. However big, he determined, it could kill them without even trying.

Quinn, he thought of his baby brother, *if you ever consider becoming a sailor when you grow up, be a merchant not a hunter!*

The fear that gripped him held on tighter than anything he'd ever felt. Worse than the moment his father left. Nothing then—not the yelling, the crying, and not even the slamming door from his memory—filled him with such bone chilling terror. His foot halted its rhythmic tapping.

Stillness.

"Sir," he said, fumbling for Aifric's arm. He couldn't take his eyes from the leviathan. "Sir?"

As usual, Aifric knew what Marek was thinking. "Aye, she's a monstrous rogue," he said in a calm voice, though his words were anything but comforting. He lowered his head to look Marek in the eyes. "Only once have I seen the like. She swamped three attack boats before receiving the deathblow. Broke about a thousand harpoons bringing her up." The skin under Aifric's left eye twitched rapidly. "Damn devil, she was," he laughed. Marek shivered, wondering if his uncle was a touch insane, and gripped the gunnel tight, clinging to his own sanity. Marek's knuckles were faintly white under the outer layer of the suit.

"But I wouldn't worry none, lad," Aifric said. He sat back and turned his head to the side until his neck popped. Maybe he saw tension on Marek's face, or maybe he was just finishing his story, but he went on. "Back in those days we had different techniques to bring'n 'em up. For instance, we never used bait. That's the kicker. Mayhap some bigger vessels were doing it then, but us smaller ships hadn't a clue it was go'n on. We relied on a lucky strike to get us the kill."

He scrunched his eyebrows, looking ahead of them, and turned to the oarsmen. "We're going off course, men! Starboard, hold!" The men on the right lifted their oars out of the water, taking in deep breaths as they rested.

The kettle was so loud Aifric had to shout over the sound of boiling water for the men in the aft part of the boat to hear him. After a few seconds, with only half the men rowing, their bearing was straight once more.

"Starboard, pull! Heave to with a will, men!" Some of them shouted as they took up their rowing. The attack boat planed over the water, leaving a considerable wake behind them.

"Bait, sir?" It was all Marek could force himself to say through tightly clenched teeth.

"Aye, lad. Bait. Our biggest challenge back then was getting 'em to show us their bellies. That's where they're soft, ya see. It's where our harpoons could do some damage." Aifric jabbed an imaginary spear at Marek's face. He flinched and immediately felt a little foolish. He made out a few chuckles over the sound of the kettle.

"The leviathan, she hates to breach. Can't stand air on their eyes, you see. It makes 'em crazy." Aifric glanced back at the oarsmen and shouted, "Don't slow now, men! We're getting close!" Some of the younger oarsmen were starting to slack, unaccustomed to long stretches of labor, their pulls getting shorter and shorter. But Aifric's shout gave them the encouragement to dig deep and row with all their might.

They were pulling quickly ahead of their prey now. Not *far*, but several boat-lengths for certain. The captain was even further ahead and still rowing.

"That's where the bait comes in," Marek said. It wasn't so

much a question as a way to get his uncle talking. Oddly, he felt less anxious listening to the man's voice. Aifric's once twitchy eye twinkled with the light of knowing, and he gave Marek a playful pat on his chest with the back of his fingers.

"We'd tie a rotting piece of flesh to a dry chunk of drift-wood and let the smell attract 'em. You see, lad, their heads are like massive blocks of granite, broad and square with eyes high on the sides. But their mouths are low, near the bottom. For the leviathan to take the bait without exposing her eyes to air, she be need'n to turn upside down to take it."

Marek saw the puzzle pieces fit into place as the first mate related his tale. It was a genius plan. "That's when she shows her belly to the harpoons!" he said, excitement over-riding the last of his anxiety.

"Right you are, lad," Aifric agreed with a wicked smile. The massive plume of white mist seemed to overtop them by hundreds of feet. "Right you are."

CHAPTER NINE

Rowan studied the kettle as his attack boat rowed past. It was a wild boil—the bubbles large, fierce, and deafening. He could no longer hear the slap of the oars. The heat coming off it nearly choked him as he breathed it in, the air-born salt stinging the back of his throat.

He looked below the boil to the faint, dark shape, black and ominous, beneath the water. The unfathomable size of the submerged leviathan would have made his jaw drop if his teeth hadn't been clenched so tight. *Stagnation, it's bigger than any beast I've ever seen.*

Rowan prayed. *Abandinus preserve us and lift our spirits from our watery graves.*

The beast was enormous. Rowan shuddered as he considered the fight he was here to pick. *What under the boiling suns have I done? Will I ever see the eyes of my baby girl again? I should have let Aifric drag me home to see her before I left.*

Rowan thought briefly of Aohd, the ship captain that had lost his mind when some of his crew failed to come back from the hunt.

Never had he come across a leviathan that made him reconsider his course, but this animal below them was different, and a part of him, though small, wanted to stop rowing and let it swim past.

He wasn't the only one to notice the beast's immense size. Several men in the boat looked up at him, the abnormal look of fear burning in their eyes. Rowan didn't say anything to them.

They continued to row.

Rowan's men looked to him not only as their leader in trade, but especially in battle. He refused to back down now. He took slow, measured breaths as the boat planed past the kettle. When he looked back, he saw a golden glimmer that chased reconsideration right out of his mind. A Devourer? *Stagnation, if that do be a Devourer...*

"Face masks on, men. I know ya hate 'em, but I'd rather not explain to yer wives and wenches why I brought ya back more grotesque than when I took ya." The men grumbled, Kier and Ennis in particular, but the more veteran sailors on his crew, Mannix and Regan, obeyed the captain's orders without complaint. Rowan followed his own demands, setting the example for his crewmen.

He reached back and pulled the hood over his head, leaving his face exposed. Before he tightened the neck straps, he tucked his long auburn hair back behind his ears and shoulders then lifted the faceplate to cover his eyes and nose, aligning the breather hole with his mouth. As the dragonhide rested over his eyes, it became completely transparent. He smiled at the marvelous gift of this magical suit.

"Now," he bellowed through the mask. Tiny slits opened to release the sound of his voice. "If'n ya don't get me ahead of this monster in the next twenty seconds, I'll be throw'n ya overboard as fodder to slow 'em while *I* get this boat in place myself. Now row for all you're worth, lads. We'll be mak'n a fortune off this kill!" He breathed in, the slits opening to allow air in past the mask.

Whether it was the threat that made them row faster or the promise of riches, the men dug deep, finding the strength within to push forward. Before Rowan knew it, they were ahead of the leviathan by a considerable margin.

He looked behind them to find Aifric's boat right on their heels. *Stagnation, the man is good.* He'd purposefully stacked his own boat with the stronger oarsmen and burdened the first mate with the incumbent boy. Yet Aifric still kept pace. Rowan respected that, but he didn't like it one bit.

Rowan *had* to be the first one to the point. He just *had* to.

Normally, he'd have stopped at their current location and set up the bait. They were far enough ahead, but he wanted to go a little farther and give himself more time to watch the kettle advance closer and closer until it was time to strike. It was a gamble, though. The leviathan could go cold before scenting Old Leary's finest. But he was willing to take the risk, and smiled inwardly as he imagined it.

"Come on, men! Row fer yer lives! Row!"

After another fifty feet, he couldn't wait any longer. His body vibrated with pent up energy. This was his moment. This is what he was made for, why he was born.

"Hold!" he shouted over the raging boil. "Stop yer row'n, damn yer hides. Bring us about. Berit, get that bait in the water, on the double." His body quivered with excitement.

Quick, sharp splashes followed the bait overboard. Rowan couldn't watch. He had to keep his eyes on the oncoming prey. Reaching down to unfasten his harpoon, he savored the familiar feel of wood in his hands.

The shaft was made of stonewood, a very dense, hearty wood. Most harpoons were made to be light and agile, but Rowan had wanted one that could hit the leviathan harder than normal. The razor-sharp tip with its cruelly hooked triple-barbs along the side reflected sunlight as he raised it into the air.

"Get yer weapons, men. We've only got one chance at this." They stored their oars between the seats and took up their harpoons. Aifric's boat pulled alongside theirs, the cabin boy, Marek, sitting next to him at the bow. The boy's face, white as the steam cloud, showed through the lad's mask.

Shouting to be heard over the oncoming boiling water, Rowan greeted his first mate with a wink. "Today, men, the god of the sea dies!" He held aloft his harpoon, brandishing it so all the men could see. Cheers rang out from both attack boats, every man hooting and hollering with battle lust.

"To the depths with her!" Aifric shouted back.

"Not the depths, my friend," Rowan corrected. "The markets!" Men cheered even louder as they imagined the gold they'd earn bringing this beast ashore.

"Positions!" Rowan yelled. The attack boats rowed away from each other—

not too far, but equal distance from the bait so the leviathan would come up between them—then turned parallel to face the oncoming kettle.

The steam cloud was ten boat-lengths away and approaching fast. Rowan stood on the narrow bench, one foot on the bow, harpoon resting on his shoulder.

This was the moment he lived for. In less time than it took for him to piss, the leviathan would be on him. He took long, humid breaths, one after the other, readying himself to throw.

Come, foul demon! I'll show you the current to hell!

Rowan watched the swell of water forced over the leviathan's massive form come closer and closer. He steadied himself, ready for his boat to rock as it met the bow.

But the swell never hit.

Only a solid wall of hot, humid steam enveloped them. It blinded him in whiteness. He couldn't see farther than a couple feet. The men next to him murmured, confused.

"Stagnation!" Rowan growled through the haze. He lowered his harpoon and unfastened his faceplate. "Bloody, damned, coral-kissing, storm-cursed—" the swearing continued in his head, but Rowan hesitated speaking the worst of them aloud. Disappointment bled from every pore of his body, yet his feeling of despair could not wipe away with a brush of a sleeve.

"What's happening, Captain?" one of the oarsmen asked in a shaky voice. Rowan was too angry to respond, but Berit was ready with an answer.

"Leviathans can't stay on top of the water too long or their own body heat burns them up. The damned fool beast went cold. No tell'n if she'll ever resurface."

"Does it happen often?" another oarsman asked.

"As often as a double eclipse," Berit responded. The hesitation afterward hung heavy in the salty air as the rest of the men pondered the meaning of the statement.

This hunt was over, and Rowan had nobody to blame but himself. He should never have waited so long.

CHAPTER
TEN

Rowan had only seen a leviathan go cold twice in all the years he'd been a hunter. Anticipating this happening hardly ever crossed his mind. They'd been on the water so long without a sighting that the excitement of finding their first leviathan in months drove him to ignore everything he learned at the feet of his first commander, Fergus Culkin.

Rowan hurled his harpoon to the opposite end of the boat, the shaft audibly vibrating from the impact. Several men fell against the gunnel to keep from getting gored.

Water still boiled, he saw, staring out at the ocean, but the circumference of the kettle diminished in size with every second. The noise of it faded as the bubbles moved farther and farther away. By the time it passed the boat entirely, it was only a faint gurgle and the steam cloud was almost completely transparent.

Bait bobbed in the water like the lonely flotsam of a sunken wreck.

Rowan sat dejected on the bow of the attack boat. *Abandinus, take me! How could I have been such a fool?* He'd heard of the prideful falling to their lusts, even experienced it himself on occasion, but never to this extreme.

Scald me; I should have stayed where I was. Why did I have to keep rowing? Why? This did be our chance to get rich beyond anything we could'a dreamed of! It could'a been a Devourer, for Abandinus' sake!

Because ya did act the fool! A voice in his head replied. *A stone-head fool!*

From across the glassy sea, Aifric shouted Rowan's name and held out his hands in a questioning gesture. Rowan just shrugged his shoulders.

"What ya think'n, Captain?" Berit asked, his voice low. No doubt the man felt nervous asking. Rowan's anger had never been too tightly held. The sound of murmuring quieted as they waited for their captain's response.

He looked at each of his crew in turn. What he said next would determine the course of their hunt. A strange thought came to him as he looked in their eyes. When he'd first seen the leviathan under the water, the sheer magnitude of the creature actually had him considering turning around and abandoning the hunt, but greed had gotten the better of him. Was this a second chance to get his men away from a fight they might not win?

"Get that bait out of the water," he ordered. Several men snatched their oars and set them in the oarlocks. "Old Leary can put it back in his barrels," he said, turning to face them. The tenseness in Rowan's muscles began to relax. He hadn't been this calm since he sat alone in his cabin. His shoulders slumped slightly and he breathed in a deep cleansing breath. "No point leav'n the drift-wood either, I'll be need'n it fer the next round. And somebody fetch my harpoon."

Berit gave the order, and the men turned the boat towards the bait. One of the oarsmen retrieved the deadly spear and tossed it, shaft first, to his captain who snatched it deftly from the air.

Aifric's boat drifted close enough to hear, so he addressed

them as well. The cabin boy, Marek, sat with a disappointed, concerned look on his youthful face. A stab of regret hit him again. Stagnation, he'd have liked to show the whelp a story come to life.

Rowan needed to say something that would buoy their spirits. Too many of his men either looked down at their feet, or stared forlornly out over the water.

"Listen up!," Rowan said over the murmurs and complaints of his crewmen. He pulled back his shoulders and straightened his spine, standing a little taller on the bow of the boat. He slapped the shaft of his spear in his hand with a loud *thwack* while he waited for them to look his way. "I know how bad ya wanted this kill, lads. Wanted to feel the harpoons leave your hands. To conquer a beast so evil hell itself can't contain it." Marcas and Connal, Jannon and Desmond, and many more of the men looked up at him with interest, though others still looked down into the water.

"Lucky for us, the sea do be filled with monsters that need kill'n." A lonely whoop from Aifric's boat echoed off the water. It sounded like Desmond, but nobody took up his encouraging cry. Many were still watching the sea as the roiling boil settled to more of a soft fizz as the leviathan swam deeper and further away.

"We do be hunters." He said confidently. One method of helping the crew know how to behave was to show them. "We've always been hunters. We've seen leviathans take upwards of twenty or thirty harpoons an' keep on swimm'n, and we just kept on hunt'n." Some of those distracted men turned to look at him. He had their attention, now he needed to give them encouragement.

"It's who we are, lads. It's what we were made for." Rowan fixed his eyes on the more frustrated of his men. "This do be the first time many of ya have seen a leviathan go cold, and I can assure ya, we'll see this again in the years to come, but we can't let it take our fire away from us." Mannix and Jannon nodded their heads in agreement. "Stagnation, we'll have more leviathans go cold over the years to come than yer will'n to admit. But Abandinus will'n, we'll hunt down every one of those god-forsaken monsters and slay 'em like the devils they are!"

He stabbed at the air with his harpoon. Not every voice cried out with eagerness, hope, but many of them did. That was enough for him, though, because emotions were contagious. If they didn't feel the excitement now, they would soon. By now the kettle had calmed completely and the last few wisps of steam were fading away like a forgotten memory.

"Nothing can stop us, lads! Nothing can keep the crew of the *Slayer of the Sea* from finding what we want. We'll bloody our hands on—"

Boiling water erupted from between the boats like a fountain of sweltering death, and from its midst rose the devil herself. Charcoal grey and coarse as a granite cliff, the leviathan soared high. A screeching bellow permeated the air like the death cry of a thousand children.

An intense heat blasted Rowan's entire being as the massive body of the leviathan twisted as the force of its momentum carried it higher and higher out of the water, baring its armored fins and the giant row of ragged spikes tracing along its spine.

In the attack boat, time slowed. Rowan turned toward the geyser that loomed over him like the shadow of oncoming torment. He didn't think. There was no time for thinking. He felt the threat the instant it breached the water. Rowan lifted the harpoon over his shoulder. As he yelled out his cry of challenge, he hurled the heavy weapon with as much strength as he could the instant the leviathan's belly came into view.

He never saw the harpoon hit its target, but a nagging fear told him he'd miscalculated the speed of its rotation. A fountain of heat scorched his skin as it misted his exposed face. Sure enough, he heard the *twang* of metal on rock over the crashing waves as the harpoon lanced the beast's iron-hard scales.

In an instant, time sped back to normal, and the boat rocked violently. Rowan felt his footing slip as his perch shifted beneath him, and he twisted his body around to fall *inside* the boat instead of out. He landed on his stomach between the seats of his attack boat. Boiling water cascaded over the hunters as the force of the leviathan's breach sent it spraying in every direction. Rowan hid his face in the crook of his arm. The oarsmen cried out in shock and terror as they witnessed a spectacle never before seen or heard of in the annals of history.

Rowan heard a loud *thunk* resonate through the wood as something heavy landed beside him in the boat, but he had no time to wonder what it could be.

He lifted his head barely in time to see the monster's tail cut its way out of the water, completely exposing its entire body to the air before it fell back into the ocean belly side up. The long, coarse spikes along its spine poised to stab the churning water beneath it.

In an instant of terror, he saw Aifric's attack boat positioned directly beneath the descending creature's blocky head. His heart sank into his stomach as the sickening crunch of wood resonated over the sound of splashing water.

He opened his mouth to scream, but nothing escaped his lips as the sea rose up before him. A blue-grey wave, tall as ten men and impregnable as a fortress's outer wall engulfed his attack boat. The wave fell like a hammer's blow, slamming his head against the bottom of the vessel with greater force than anything he could have imagined.

As the curtain of shadow fell over his consciousness, a vision of brilliant, sparkling blue eyes blinking in the sun danced before him.

Asy!

CHAPTER FIVE

Can misfortune ever turn out for our good? I cannot accurately answer such a question. The needs of each are his and the lessons life teaches are tailored to fit the individual. But I'll say this for myself. Never have I passed through fire and come out weaker than I entered. The refineries of Abandinus's watery forge have tempered me into a tougher man, a hardened sailor, and an indomitable killer.

—Fergus Culkin, captain of the Domnall, *leviathan ship of the first class, personal ship of the king*

CHAPTER
ELEVEN

*A*bandinus *preserve me and lift my spirit from my watery grave!*

Preserve me!

Please!

Marek repeated the prayer over and over in the seconds he floundered under the water's tempestuous surface. Aside from the scalding heat on his skin and the suffocating pressure on his chest, he could feel his body spinning beneath the crashing waves, pushing him deeper and deeper. He fought against it. Kicked for all he was worth. Not once did he resign himself to death.

The spinning stopped.

Air! I need air! Abandinus preserve me, I can't breathe! I can't—

Something knocked against his head. Pressure was the only thing to register in his brain. A couple seconds later, something grabbed him by the shoulders, and he felt his body lifting forcibly upward. The darkness pressing against his closed eyes grew lighter and lighter until, suddenly, his head broke the surface of the ocean. Bathed in bright sunlight, he gasped in the sweet breath of life and choked on salt water as it stole a way into his lungs.

"Wha—? Who—?" he stammered, as his arms flailed and legs kicked to keep himself afloat. Strong hands spun him around, and the face of Desmond—cloudy and almost featureless through the semi-transparent mask—appeared before him like a vision of Abandinus himself.

"I gotcha, boy. I gotcha," Desmond said through the slits of his mask. Marek reached desperate hands out to his savior, his eager fingers gripping the older man's leather suit. He pulled himself closer to Desmond and even tried to wrap his legs around his torso so as not to slip back under the water, panic overwhelming his senses.

"No need to pull me down, boy. Relax. *Relax!*" But Marek was too frightened to listen, and his grip became iron as he found safety in anchoring himself to the man.

Suddenly, his vision spun and his body lost muscle control. A ringing in his ears began, quiet at first but louder with each passing second. A dull ache on the side of his head told Marek what had happened, and he was shocked at what the man had done. However, the fear of drowning fled him entirely. Desmond grasped him around the middle, and somehow the man found a heavy piece of debris from the crushed attack boat to hold on to.

"Sorry, Marek," Desmond said, his breathing heavy and laden with exhaustion. "First rule of survival... don't let the man you're saving... drown you." Marek heard the words, but didn't consider responding. *Stagnation, my head hurts.*

He looked out across the water, blinking to clear away the disorientation and vertigo. When it cleared, Marek's heart sank at the scene around him. Pieces of his boat were scattered in all directions. Some of the oarsmen, like Desmond, were using them to stay afloat, while others... others just floated.

Still.

Unmoving.

Lingering panic seemed to press even harder on his chest, and the feeling of claustrophobia and excruciating heat robbed him of his ability to breathe. Something was covering his nose and mouth. His hands reached for the mask covering his face, frantically attempting to rip it off. He had to get it off! He had to get it—

Strong hands suppressed his clamoring fingers and a calm voice in his ear erased much of his terror with just a single reminder.

"You don't want to do that, Lad," Desmond's voice said assuredly, "this water will melt the skin right off yer face. Just wait a bit and it'll cool down before ya know it." He didn't shout. He didn't scold. He said it as though he were calmly telling a child water would cure his thirst.

Marek's breathing normalized and sense returned to him. *I'm not gonna die,* he told himself, *I can breathe just fine. I can breathe.*

A large piece of wood drifted nearby and Marek reached a hand out to take it, allowing Desmond the relief of letting him go. As his hand touched the splintered wood, his vision flashed and the memory of a demon with blood red eyes, covered in spikes, scales, and razor-sharp fins loomed over him.

What if it comes back? What if it attacks again?

But he knew the beast would not return. Uncle Aifric's lesson on leviathans burning to death reassured him of that.

"Thank you, Desmond," Marek said, after he'd managed to dispel the awful memory. He looked the man in the eye, trying to convey his sincerity. What would have happened if Desmond hadn't been here to pull him up? He didn't want to think any further on that. Much of his panic was now gone, but anxiety still pumped through him. He supposed that was normal though, considering the circumstances.

"Don't mention it, boy." He gave Marek a quick smile

before adjusting his grip on the wooden plank, before turning to examine the sea around him. "Sorry I had to hit ya."

Marek looked in the direction Desmond had turned. A miniscule amount of relief calmed him somewhat when he saw the captain's attack boat rowing their way. But something about it felt wrong to Marek. Where was Captain Donchaad? Wouldn't he be at the head of the boat? He couldn't possibly be...

The sound of groaning distracted Marek, and he turned to see a man treading water. He didn't seem to be panicked. He wasn't flailing nor thrashing, just groaning. But all around him the water looked cloudy and scarlet.

"Aifric?" Marek muttered under his breath, recognizing the man's features.

"Aifric!"

Marek let go of the plank to swim to him, but he had no energy to cover the distance. He returned his grip to his lifeline and began to pull himself one-armed through the brine toward his uncle. Desmond followed right behind him. He must've heard Marek's yell.

"Aifric, hold on!" Marek said.

Aifric turned to look at him and the paleness of his face and deadness of his eyes shook Marek to his core. His uncle was white as a ghost. Struggling to keep afloat, Aifric's lips dipped beneath the waterline. Marek pulled him back up but in doing so dipped beneath the water himself. He wasn't expecting that to happen and inadvertently sucked in hot, salty water that scalded his throat and lungs. He coughed and spluttered as he resurfaced and cried out for help.

"Desmond! Desmond, help me!" Before he knew it, Desmond was at his side and together they surrounded the injured man and grabbed him under the arms to hold him above the waterline.

Water that rippled red with Aifric's blood.

"Over here!" Desmond called out to the rescue boat. "The first mate's hurt!" Marek looked to see if the men on board heard them and saw Berit standing at the bow pointing in their direction.

"Hang on, sir. Help is coming. Help is—" Marek's voice cracked for the first time. His emotions were finally catching up to him. Seeing this man—this strong, capable, kindly man—in such condition was disturbing and filled him with emotions he never thought he'd ever feel again. *Don't do it, Uncle. Don't leave!*

As much as he loathed his father for abandoning him, Marek had loved the time he'd spent with him. *Now Aifric? Will he leave me too?* He stopped that line of thinking before it could go too far. He was not going to let himself become the victim of another tragedy. He couldn't sail that ship again.

"Just hold on," he whispered, laying his head against Aifric's. The man was so weak he could barely hold his chin out of the water.

Berit pulled the boat up next to him and Desmond. Three of the oarsmen reached down to take hold of Aifric's dragonhide suit. Together they lifted him out of the sea, the gunnel nearly dipping below the water line. Marek shuddered, knowing he was about to witness the wound that had tainted the water around them. Sure enough, the ragged muscle of Aifric's calf emerged, reminding Marek of the rotting leviathan flesh Leary pulled from the barrel an hour earlier, only here ragged bits of pulverized bone poked through the shredded skin and muscle.

Marek gasped in shock, his anxiety multiplying tenfold.

Aifric's weakened body flopped into the boat like a fish exhausted from fighting the line. Marek reached for the gunnel and pulled himself up to see what was going on. Berit had the belt from his discarded britches and was wrapping it tightly above Aifric's knee, the stretched leather acting as a tourniquet to stop the bleeding.

But that wasn't the only thing that disturbed Marek. All the men in the boat were bleeding from somewhere on their exposed faces. Bloody noses were the most common, but a few gashed foreheads, and even a bandaged eye, littered the oarsmen's countenances.

Then, underneath them all, stretched down the middle of the craft, lay the captain. His head was propped on a coil of line, safely above the several inches of water that filled the bottom of the boat, his face masked in red.

Somebody grabbed Marek and pulled him in. Desmond soon joined them. Marek unbuckled his mask and pulled it off his face inhaling deeply. The perspiration on his skin cooled instantly, tingling his skin. Feeling considerably less stressed now that he was safe in the attack boat, and despite all the pain surrounding him, he leaned back and closed his eyes.

"Anybody else still alive out there, Desmond?" a crewman asked. Marek recognized the voice but wasn't sure the man's name. He was one of those that tried not to get close to others.

"Abandinus willing, I sure hope so," Desmond replied. Marek peeked through closed lids just enough to see him smooth wet hair away from his eyes and give his head a shake to clear out his ears. Marek perked up when he caught a glimpse of movement from the edge of his vision.

"There's one!" Marek said, bolting upright and pointing to a large patch of splintered planks.

"That looks like Mannix!" Desmond said. His voice cracked as he leaned out over the side of the boat.

"Turn the damn boat around," Berit ordered. "We have to get as many as we can. The living first!"

"We can't leave the others," a crewman stated.

"We leave nobody! Not even the dead." Berit grumbled the last part as he looked out over the splinter-strewn waves. Too many of those larger *splinters* bobbed a bit too unnaturally.

CHAPTER TWELVE

Rowan groaned, struggling to breathe from a weight pressing against his side. A rhythmic pounding at his temples felt like something trying to beat memories from his brain. He rubbed his eyes with his palms and felt the warmth of his own skin against his eyelids. Vaguely, he wondered when he'd removed his dragonhide suit.

Light shone directly on his closed lids, amplifying the strain on his already aching head. Rowan shied away from the sun's rays. *Is that Belinus, or Belinos?* Soft, dry linens cradled the back of his head and neck, the strangeness of it breaking down the bulkhead of his memory's hold, and suddenly he could remember every detail of the leviathan attack up until the massive wave unbalanced him, knocking him unconscious.

I can't believe my own eyes. Did that leviathan really breach the cursed water? Though he questioned his own memory, he could recall with perfect clarity the spiked tail hovering over him like an emissary of death.

He forced himself to wake completely, and the blurred outlines of his surroundings slowly sharpened into his own cabin aboard the *Slayer of the Sea*. He sat up, testing the movements of his body for additional injuries. Other than a few stiff joints, he seemed to be fine.

Stagnation, I should be dead. We all should.

He groaned as he sat up, bare to the waist. The throb in his head slowly subsided as blood rushed from his scalp down through his neck and into his body. He let out a sigh of relief. *A drink about now, do be a grand idea.* But as he looked around his room for a full bottle of whiskey, or even a half-empty one, the presence of an unfamiliar cot laid out over the chests lining the bulkhead caught his attention.

A man lay there, his body still as a corpse.

Rowan swung his legs over the edge of the bed, intent on finding out who shared his room. Something heavy slid from his bed and landed solidly on the floor with an echoing thud. Curiously, he looked down by his bare feet.

A greyish-brown leviathan scale the size of a dinner plate lay there. Gold veins like bolts of lightning streaked through the surface. For a second there, he'd forgotten to breathe. *Abandinus, what games do ya be play'n?* He caught a breath then bent over and picked it up, but his grip was too weak. *Stagnation, it's heavy!*

A piece of leviathan armor this size was completely new to Rowan. He'd harvested hundreds of thousands of scales over the years he'd spent on the sea, but never had he found one this big or with this much gold in it. In fact, he'd only killed two Devourers in his life and none of them had gold streaks this intricate. Neither had he found one that could have served as an anchor.

He turned it over to examine it from all angles, eager to see if the back had any—

His breath caught and this time he wasn't able to loosen his throat right away. He had to swallow hard to loosen and moisten it, disbelief clouding his thought processes. *This can't be!*

Light streaming in through his windows glistened off a brilliant sheet of solid, yellow gold. He was so shocked he nearly dropped it back to the floor. A memory of seeing the glint of gold under the boiling water of the kettle floated to the forefront of his mind.

He knew then that this beast was indeed a Devourer. Maybe even the largest Devourer in the ocean. He never could have believed one would consume so much wealth.

Where did the boil'n thing come from? How did it get here? He idly scratched his head, thinking.

My harpoon must have dislodged it. Only chance could explain how it landed in his boat. *Well, mayhap someth'n good came out of this after all.* He suddenly remembered the man across the room. Whatever was wrong with him, he knew, wasn't good. How many others had sacrificed for the acquisition of this singular scale? Surely not just the one man. The Devourer scale suddenly felt a lot heavier.

Rowan stood, dropping the scale carelessly on the bed linens with a soft thump, and shuffled over to the cot, looking down on his first mate. A flashing image of Aifric's boat positioned beneath the leviathan reminded him of what happened.

Aifric!

Blood suddenly rushed to his head, his ears ringing with the pressure. His hand shook as he reached for his friend, unsure if he should touch him. *Not you, my friend. After all these years work'n to keep ya in line, I can't be losing ya now.*

He put a hand on Aifric's chest and felt the gentle rise and fall of someone deeply asleep. He looked rather peaceful, but when he gently touched the man's forehead, it practically burned his hand with fever-heat. *Stagnation!*

Rowan traced the length of Aifric's body with his eyes, looking for the injury that must have caused the infection burning him up inside and out. Immediately he noticed the premature end to his mate's left leg.

He lifted the linen sheet. Sure enough, Aifric's leg had been amputated just below the knee. A wave of heat, fueled by guilt and anger flooded down his spine, filling his arms and legs like canteens of hot tea. Rowan had done this. He was to blame for Aifric's condition. But there were other men on that boat. Did any of them come away with missing limbs too? What about the boy?

"Marek?" The mumbled name slurred faintly through Aifric's lips like honey from a comb, slow and gelatinous. Rowan had to think to recognize the intended question, but not long.

"He's fine, mate," Rowan said, his voice scratchy. He coughed into his fist. Stagnation, he had no idea if the boy had made it. A tear tugged at his eye thinking what may have happened to the whelp. But Aifric seemed to be even more concerned than he was. Telling his first mate anything but "all is well" was like plunging a dagger into the man's heart. Injured men always needed some hope to hold onto. "I did see him a moment ago scooping water out'a the attack boats. Damn good cabin boy, that one is, just as ya said he'd be."

A crook at the corner of Aifric's mouth told Rowan his story was accepted. Aifric took a long, stuttered breath and released it with a beleaguered sigh. As long as infection didn't overtake the man, Aifric would be just fine, but Rowan had never felt a fever that hot before. Never. He wiped away the sheen of sweat from Aifric's brow with the hem of his linen sheet before turning away. Now for that bottle. Old Leary must have one down in the galley—

A faint creak came from the front of the cabin. He turned to see the door slowly open a crack. A youthful face peeked in. Marek. *Abandinus preserve me, he made it after all.*

"Captain?" the boy said hesitantly, his shy voice nearly a squeak. He looked unhurt. His clothes were much the same as before, but the trousers were missing a tear in the knee. Marek must have changed his pants. How long had Rowan been out?

"Marek, lad," Rowan said softly, glancing toward Aifric's sleeping form. "Glad to see ya made it back." Rowan shuffled over to the door, opening it wide enough to let the boy stumble inside. Marek looked small. Smaller than before. Fragile even.

"Me too," he said quietly, looking around the room. His gaze stopped on Aifric's sleeping form. "I thought I was gonna drown for certain, sir. Either that or get eaten alive."

"Well, I'm glad ya didn't. It's bad luck to lose yer cabin boy on his first trip," he said with a quiet, insincere laugh. The chuckle was short lived. "Aifric didn't come out of it too good." He paused a moment to see how the boy reacted. Marek simply nodded. *He's a tough one.* "Who, uh, who did we lose? I can't believe we all came out of this alive."

Marek looked at the floor, his eyes either unable or unwilling to meet Rowan's. He didn't speak, not without some encouragement.

"I'd ask my first mate, Marek," Rowan prompted, "but as ya can see he's in no too good a shape for give'n reports." He paused a moment to let Marek respond in his own time. *Poor lad, I should never have let Aifric convince me to allow him on board.* Rowan had little time or patience for softness. This was a tough life, living at sea hunting leviathans, and he needed Marek to be tough.

Rowan cleared his throat. "I'd rather not waste time send'n ya for Berit, so I do be need'n ya to answer as soon as yer able. Can ya do that for me, lad?" Rowan lifted the boy's chin to show him his most reassuring, yet urgent, smile.

The boy met his eyes and nodded. "Six dead, sir," he said, standing straight and stealing another quick glance at Aifric.

Rowan's heart sank to his ankles. *Six!* One crewman dead was devastating enough, but *six*!? The room suddenly felt smaller, darker. The wood planks around him looked an awful lot like the coffin he'd laid his wife to rest in.

"Who, lad?" he asked darkly. "Who's dead?" Rowan knelt, resting a hand on the boy's shoulder. A part of him expected Marek to pull back from his touch. They hadn't been close by any means, but if anything, the kid stood straighter.

"Well," Marek said, "there's Gaf and Samuel. Also, Breye. We brought most of them back on board, but, uh, we couldn't find Breye's body." The boy bowed his head as though he'd failed. Rowan squeezed his shoulder gently to tell him he'd done no such thing.

Breye was the kind of sailor that laughed at everything, funny or not. He always made Rowan feel like a comedic genius. Gaf had a litany of curse words to hand out to anybody who dared disturb him while he was sleeping even though waking the man had been nigh impossible. And Samuel was a storyteller. Though young, he'd had countless tales to impart to anybody who'd listen. Most did and they'd loved every impractical tale.

Rowan felt a stab to the chest remembering each man. All had been relatively new recruits. He wanted so much to make good sailors out of them, but...

"Also, Colm, Oisin, and Marcas. We, we—" Marek's body began to shudder, his chest and shoulders jerking with quick sharp breaths. Stagnation, the boy had no business dealing in so much death. Rowan felt the failure deep in his soul.

CHAPTER
THIRTEEN

"Spit it out, boy," he said, patting gently on Marek's shoulder. "Once it's out, it can't hurt ya any more." Rowan wished that were true. Sometimes pain never left and memories never faded. All he could do was drink away whatever pain and memory haunted him, and even that rarely worked. Drunk or not, the faces of his dead wife and abandoned baby continued to haunt him. Maybe Marek wouldn't be haunted by these six men. Rowan hoped he wouldn't, but their faces would surely haunt him. *Add them to the damned list.*

"We only found parts of them, captain," Marek mumbled in a rush, though he didn't take his eyes from the deck.

Rowan blinked and scratched his beard. He opened his mouth to say something, but nothing came to mind. It was too much, way too much. These last three names had been veterans, had been with him for years, had been close friends. He looked out the door at the bright white sails billowing with wind. Their faces seemed to appear one after another on the pure backdrop of canvas. Water began welling up in his eyes and before long he couldn't see clearly. He feared if he blinked, it'd wash away their faces from his memory. Rowan knew the thought was ridiculous.

After a respectful minute, he steeled himself and blinked away a tear. This was a hard life. Rowan needed to be hard. *Caring too much makes ya weak*, he reminded himself. He couldn't think about them and stay strong for what was left of his crew. He just couldn't.

"And the injured?" he asked brusquely, not allowing himself time to ruminate on the dead. *What's done do be done, but stagnation, I did never lose so many at once.*

"Mannix lost an eye," Marek explained, unexpectedly smiling and letting out a mirthful laugh. "He says he absorbed a leviathan spike inside it and now claims he can see twice as good with the other, but Leary found bits of wood lodged in the socket. Besides him and yourself," Marek hesitated looking over to Aifric, "just bumps, bruises, and a few cuts for everyone."

Rowan breathed in *another* sigh of relief. He was getting tired of those.

"Oh," Marek said feeling tenderly at his face, "most of the men had minor burns on their faces from the hot water."

Well, that wasn't exactly good, but Rowan knew all too well that it could have been much worse.

A commotion on deck pulled Marek's attention to the door. Rowan didn't rush to see what it was. He wanted to let Marek know that he had his captain's full attention. It was the least he could give the lad.

Abandinus, watch over those men for me.

"Um, sir?" Marek asked, shifting his feet and wiping his hands on his shirt.

"What is it?"

"There's a ship at our starboard," Marek replied, pointing to the door. "It looks like a Privileged vessel."

"Privileged vessel?" Rowan asked, raising an eyebrow. He felt a slight flutter in his middle. Looking out the door for himself, Rowan couldn't see past the mainsail. "Are you sure?"

"It's waving the royal seal," Marek said. There was no questioning look to the boy. He was definitely sure of what he'd seen.

Thoughts of his fallen crew fled his mind, and a wave of panic and anger took its place. Rowan flew to his trunk and opened the lid, his muscles aching with every shift. Not really caring what clothes he put on, he replaced his cut-off rag shorts with a pair of pants rolled up above the ankle and covered his upper torso with a button-free white linen shirt with baggy sleeves.

Abandinus, preserve me from fools and thieves!

He pulled his hair back into a queue and tied it with a strand of leather and retrieved the scale with its sheet of heavy, polished gold. *After everything I did lose today, I can't be lose'n this.* Rowan could see a vague reflection of himself in the yellow ore. For an instant the faces of the men he'd lost replaced his own. An unsettling fear linked his memories of these men with this invaluable relic. If he ever lost it, would he forget about his men? He hoped he'd never find out.

He looked over at Aifric lying silent and still on his cot. Doubt ate a hole in his gut. Aifric was as strong a man as Rowan had ever met, but an infection as hot as Aifric's would take a miracle to cure. *If ever I did need a miracle, now do be that time.* Carefully, gingerly, Rowan lifted his first mates left arm, the one closest to the bulkhead. Aifric groaned, but didn't resist as Rowan slid the heavy scale under his arm, gold side up—the smooth surface being more comfortable against his bare skin.

Before Rowan left the room, he placed a hand on Aifric's chest. The throbs of his heart came faster than normal, with long pauses between beats. *Stagnation, this may be the last time I see him alive.* "Hold fast, my friend!"

He was out the door.

He knew it seemed an odd place to hide a treasure, but

most of the Privileged captains had already searched and discovered his secret places years ago. They'd never suspect a dying man to be hiding anything expensive.

From the bridge Rowan watched the massive ship approach, its five masts flying upward of thirty sails. Oh, how he knew these vessels. His memories were still sharp as ever. The royal seal flew above the gull's nest, an osprey in flight circled in gold on a field of green. She was an impressive ship.

"She do be a Privileged vessel," he said to nobody in particular.

"Aye," Berit responded, standing at the wheel. "She must be twice our size—all those masts and sails." Rowan looked at him with a sidelong glance. He hated seeing awe in his men's faces when they looked at other ships, even more when they pointed out the flaws in his. Even if it was just their size. *It ain't the size of the ship that matters.*

"But which ship is it?" Rowan asked. "Who captains this... abomination?"

"Not sure captain," Berit replied, hands steady on the wheel. "Can't see too clearly from this distance."

Rowan returned to his cabin and retrieved his looking glass. Extending the brass tubes, he held the lens to his eye. *Cutlass.* Rowan groaned audibly. This captain, he knew all too well, was a decent man, but a bit of a drunk. But who wasn't? The lieutenant commander, however, he loathed more than anything else in this world.

Abandinus, preserve us from fools and thieves!

However this encounter went, it'd be either a waste of time or a disaster for everyone on board.

"Berit?" Rowan asked, lowering the looking glass.

"Sir?"

He hated saying it, but Rowan had no choice. Evading a royal ship was a criminal offense even if he could outrun it.

"Take in the sail as soon as ya can and check our depth. Let go the anchor if possible."

"As you command, sir."

"One more thing, Berit," he said before the deck boss could carry out the order. "Send Marek for some cold, damp towels. Aifric's fever is getting out of hand."

"Of course," he said. "You'll man the wheel while I'm gone, Captain?"

"Aye, I'll man the wheel." Rowan slid the tubes together and tucked the looking glass into his waistband. "Oh, and if ya don't mind, I'll be need'n me sword as well."

PART SIX

As every brigand knows, respect for the law only needs come from those enforcing it. Anyone willing to risk lawlessness simply needs hide the misdeed from those in power. But a warning to those foolish, or brave, enough to take such risks: when the penetrating darkness of one's unlawful past meets the blinding light of discovery, the law can be as merciless as the storm-battered sea.

—Fergus Culkin, captain of the Domnall, *leviathan ship of the first class, personal ship of the king*

CHAPTER
FOURTEEN

"Captain Donchaad!" Cass Alby called, swaggering onto the deck of *The Slayer of the Sea* by way of a gangplank connecting the two ships.

Rowan scowled as he watched his old friend, trailed by a half dozen Kingmen in uniform vests of dark green with gold trim, clamber aboard his ship like a parade of waterfowl. Cass looked like a momma goose leading her young.

Some of his men wore cloth caps tied at the back and adorned their ears with silver hoops of varying sizes, but Cass's apparel was much more official, even more so than the traditional first crewman's attire. He wore a fancy coat with pressed lapels in the same colors as his goslings, but with shiny black boots on his feet, and a long slender sword strapped to his side. Rowan's jaw suddenly felt sore. He didn't realize he'd been clenching his teeth. *Abandinus preserve me, that can't possibly be a captain's badge!*

"The ship's looking fit as an old shirt," Cass said, walking over the catamaran bridge to the main deck.

The man was insufferable, loud, and domineering. Rowan despised him. Even his elevated speech drove Rowan crazy. It took everything Rowan had to keep from walking up to the man and punching him in his fool face. That and the fear of being locked in a cell for the rest of mortality.

He descended the companion ladder from the bridge where Berit stood near the wheel with steam seeming to blow out his ears, to meet the ship captain on the deck.

"It's been what, a month, since we last parted ways?" Cass's hands grasped the lapels of his officer's coat. "Ocean been good to ya? Eh?" he said with a smug wink.

This personable communication took Rowan back to the days he and Cass were novice oarsmen aboard Fergus Culkin's ship. The two men had been quite close in their early years. Ports of call all along the isles of Manks knew them as ruffians and scoundrels. The serving girls in the local taverns never seemed to get through an entire shift whenever the two were in town.

If his own reprehensible behavior then had never made Rowan regret his actions, having to put up with Cass now certainly did.

"You do be a long way from home, Cass. What brings ya way out here to the backside of forever?" Privileged vessels primarily searched for pirates and smugglers unless they were transferring precious cargo for the king or one of his favored dignitaries.

"Oh, you know me," the bastard said, feigning innocence. "Orders from the king, you know." Cass ran his hands down the lapels of his finely woven satin coat. Gold buttons complimented the expensive captain's badge. *So, he wasn't just blow'n smoke up me arse. He actually do be a captain. Well, I'll be damned if I let him know I see his fancy badge.*

Cass's show of station, no doubt meant to intimidate, didn't impress Rowan. Cass leaned in. "Between you and me," he said, "I think he just likes hearing himself give orders. I mean, who in their right mind sends an expensive ship like mine into the middle of the sea to tax poor fishing boats?" A forced chuckle belied his true feelings on the matter. "Why can't he just tax the poor bastards at the docks like every other king in the empire? You know what I mean, Rowan?"

"Yeah, right. Taxes." Rowan laughed at the absurdity of the idea. He folded his arms, ready to hear the next idiotic phrase to pass Cass's lips.

"Yes, taxes," Cass said, clearly ignoring the fact that Rowan didn't believe him. "But orders are orders," he said as though he thought the idea absurd, "and what the king wants, he gets. It's how the waves crash, you know?" He held out his hands as if there was nothing he could do about it.

"Don't I ever," Rowan said. *Abandinus preserve me. I thought the man's boast about getting his own ship was a bluff.* At other times he'd be spit'n mad about this breach of democracy. Considering his hulls were completely empty, though, it was a good excuse to hustle the boisterous fool off his ship before he could uncover Rowan's not-so-little secret.

"But do let me save ya some time, old friend. I've been out here a couple of months and there's been no leviathan in sight. It do be a travesty, I know." He turned the man around by his shoulders and began walking him back to the catamaran bridge. "I'll tell ya what, Cass, I do be sailing into the merchant's dock on Manks no later than a month from now. If you're there," they stepped over a coil of line lying in their path, "I'll be sure to let ya tax my cargo before the Dockmasters get a crack at it."

It was a shameless bribe, but maybe it would be enough to get the man off his ship. *I can't have this Kingman tax me of the one thing my men lost their lives for. They just can't.*

"Rowan," Cass said, his boots squeaking to a halt on the clean, yet cluttered, deck. "You know I can't very well steal from the king," he said admonishingly. "I certainly cannot. Besides, as a Privileged captain, it's my duty to inspect any vessel I come across, not only for taxation, but also for any general unlawful transaction. For example, I can't possibly let a slave trader pass me by without stopping him, can I?"

"Slave trader?" Rowan barked indignantly. He stepped up to his former friend leaning into Cass's face. "What's that supposed to mean?"

"I'm just making an example, Rowan, not an accusation," Cass said, holding out a placatory hand and taking a quick step back.

"Cass, you know very well I do no deal in slaves," Rowan said pulling his eyeglass from his waistband and brandishing it like a club. "It's a filthy business that I have nothing to do with."

"Of course not, old friend," Cass said, taking another step back. He gently reached for the eyeglass and slowly pressed it down, out of his face. "Of course not. The lack of evidence in *your* trial was quite convincing. The prosecution nearly hung their own key witness, they were so embarrassed." Cass laughed. *Right. Laugh all you want, you thieving bastard. You hired those prosecutors. And the witness.*

"Then why ya be bring'n it up?" Rowan asked, shaking his head. "Let the past stay in the past. I don't want it on my deck." He turned away from the man, tossing his eyeglass up on the bridge to keep him from beating the man with it. He cringed as it clinked on the planks above. *Stagnation, my lenses.*

"Because as a law man I have to anticipate everyone— merchant, fisherman, smuggler. I need to inspect your ship, Rowan. You understand, don't you? Nobody is beyond my scrutiny." He reached out to grab Rowan by the shoulder as if to say *agree with me, old friend, you know I'm right.*

Rowan spun around and swatted it away like a fly.

Inside, he boiled like a kettle, hot anger filling him with rage. He clenched his hands into fists. *Don't let the fool get under yer skin,* he told himself. Stagnation, he wanted to break

Cass's overly large nose right then and there. But Rowan held back as Cass pulled away and turned to talk with his men.

Rowan's breaths came sharp and shallow. He'd had enough of this man. Whatever he had to do to get him off his ship, Rowan would do it, even if it meant cooperating in full.

"Fine," Rowan said. "But, Cass," the man looked back at Rowan. "My first mate do be in my cabin, near death. He did tangle with a leviathan earlier today. Don't ya be wake'n him up or I swear I'll gut ya like a cuttertrout." *Stagnation, why did I say that? I should have kept my mouth shut!*

"Oh, never you worry," Cass said with a cold smile that never touched his eyes. "He won't even know my men are there." Cass looked backward over his shoulder to his men and snapped his fingers. Rowan watched them fan out across his decks like crabs looking for a rotting carcass to devour.

CHAPTER
FIFTEEN

Rowan watched as Kingmen overturned barrels, tossed coils of line, and rummaged through whatever they thought might conceal something valuable. By law, they could only tax the cargo, but nobody could stop them from plundering whatever wasn't nailed down on threat of being arrested.

It took Cass only a quarter of an hour to complete his search of the ship. Rowan's crew witnessed it all with clenched fists as they were robbed before their eyes. There was nothing abnormally special on deck to take, but a few things did slip into Privileged pockets.

Berit threatened to start throwing harpoons at every fancy coat he could see, but Rowan stopped him, explaining that they'd probably confiscate every harpoon they hurled. Steel was expensive and took too much time re-forging.

Finnian paced the deck groaning and moaning at every spilled barrel or tangled line that would have to be cleaned up. He hated messes. Finnian had been following the Kingmen step for step, cleaning up after them until the sharp tip of a polished cutlass sent him down to the forecastle to wait it all out.

At one point Old Leary burst from below decks, a stained, crusty towel in his hands and a burr in his britches.

"Stagnation, this is an outrage!" the cook barked, his enormous belly bumping into Rowan as he stomped up to him. Rowan had to regain his footing after being knocked off balance. "My galley's been turned into an utter disaster!" he bellowed, swinging a grimy spoon. "What's going on here, Captain? Why are there men crawling all over my galley? We been searched before, but this do be a bit excessive, don't it? Who ever heard of hustling a cook out of his kitchen?"

Rowan knew it was best to just let the man get it out of his system. Soon Old Leary would be as calm as a turtle. The aging chef continued grumbling until Cass whistled for Rowan to join him on the bridge. Only then did Old Leary stop, presumably when he saw Rowan's burning eyes.

Rowan could have chewed nails. He turned rigidly and approached the ladder to the bridge. He stopped there, forcing himself to keep things in perspective. *Ignore the fool and focus on acting as though ya have nothing to hide.*

Nothing to hide.

He took a deep breath and climbed the stairs, skipping every other step, and approached the intruding captain. Cass had to have noticed Rowan's rigid gait so he tried to relax. *Act natural, boil yer hide!* But he just couldn't manage it.

"Search not going too well?" Rowan asked, looking out over his ship and scratching the thick hair on his chin. *Hand down, fool. Stop yer scratch'n.* "The king's coffers a bit light these days, I presume?" Rowan risked a glance into his cabin. He felt a stab of fear when he saw Aifric's cot resting on the floor, but the man looked relatively undisturbed. His blanket was neat and unruffled.

"You presume too much, old friend," Cass replied. Berit, standing at the wheel, grunted in exasperation. Both men looked at him. Rowan wondered if Berit had a comment to follow up the gesture of disgust. "Can't we get a little privacy around here?" Cass aimed a sour expression at the deck boss. "I'm not accustomed to letting just anyone listen in on my conversations."

"With my first mate out of commission," Rowan explained as if to a child, "the deck boss do be my next in command." He gestured to the gruff man holding the stationary wheel in place. Rowan walked over to Berit and massaged the man's shoulders. "I *will* be tell'n him in council all that we do talk about. No point in send'n him off now." Berit looked over his shoulder at Rowan with an uncomfortable glare, but Rowan just winked and smiled. Cass had to have seen that, but Rowan didn't care.

"So be it," Cass said, wiping damp sweat from his brow with a crisp, white, linen handkerchief. He folded it perfectly and returned it to his breast pocket.

"Tell me about this," Cass said, signaling something from inside Rowan's cabin. One of the Kingmen came out holding the massive leviathan scale, the inside plated with solid gold. Cass took the heavy object, struggling to hold it steady, and signaled to the man to wait behind him. Rowan's heart not only stopped for an entire second, but it also sank, deflated, to the ocean floor. The one thing he feared above all others.

It's the greatest treasure I ever did find, and I doubt I'll ever be find'n another.

Rowan's shoulders fell slightly as he looked over at Berit. The avid sailor showed no sign of astonishment. Rowan knew without words the sailor knew all about the scale.

He did be with me when it fell in the boat. For sure, he'd have seen it. Probably laid it on my chest himself.

"You've seen scales before, Cass," he said, holding in his disappointment. He had to force life into his voice. Aside from the value of the gold, it was a memento reminding him of the men he'd lost and the Devourer that killed them.

Greed reflected in Cass's cold eyes as he looked longingly at the relic. "Scales, yes," Cass said gleefully, "even gold-plated scales. But this is the largest by far that I've ever seen." Despair settled on Rowan like a heavy cloud on a cool summer morning. He may never see, or even hold, that scale again.

"I'd never have believed it if I hadn't seen it with my own eyes," Cass continued. He couldn't keep his eyes off it. He looked like a man entranced. "It's more than remarkable, it's downright extraordinary."

"Not to mention, it do be mine, Cass," Rowan said, snatching the plate-sized scale out of his hand. Once again, the weight of the thing took him by surprise. *Did it get heavier in the past twenty minutes?*

"Yes, well, that's an argument for another day," Cass replied. He whistled, loud and clear, and his men on deck stopped their search immediately. Rowan let out a sigh of relief. The man was going to let him keep it after all. Cass turned to the stairs, and Rowan stepped out of his way, allowing him to pass. But before his boot hit the third step, Cass turned back to look at Rowan, eyes squinted, as though trying to see something that wasn't there.

"I have to ask you," Cass said, as though realizing something he'd been trying to remember. A narrow finger tapped lightly on his chin as he spoke. "Property taxes are the most commonly overlooked taxes by ship owners from Manks. It's difficult, you see, for the king to enforce every law he's decreed. But enforced or not, the law *is* binding, and failure to make payments can result in the seizure of property, accounts, and goods." Cass returned to the top of the steps to look him in the eye. Rowan knew what was coming, and it sickened him. Sweat beaded on his brow, and his underarms were completely soaked.

"Tell me, Captain Donchaad," Cass said, clasping his

hands behind his back and pacing the length of the bridge. "Have you paid taxes on this beautiful ship of yours?" He gestured all around him, smiling in seeming wonder at the simple yet beautiful architecture that was the *Slayer of the Sea*. "I'd surely hate to see her confiscated and incorporated into the royal fleet if you haven't."

Rowan didn't respond, his anger had reached a new high. He expected to see red steam emanating from his skin. If he said anything, he'd be hard-pressed not to explode. His feet shifted beneath him into a fencing stance and he gripped the hilt of his cutlass.

"Your silence speaks loudly, my old friend," Cass said, noticeably eyeing Rowan's hand on his hilt. "In truth, it breaks my heart." He wandered over to the wheel, pushing Berit aside. He traced his finger along the turned, rounded handles.

Through clenched teeth, Rowan made his objection. "You're not taking my ship." He wanted to believe he was current on his taxes, but Shannon—the old man managing his estate on Manks—was getting up there in age. He could easily have forgotten to pay them.

Cass cocked an eyebrow. "No. No, I'm not." He flicked the wheel from one rung to another, then back to the first. It wasn't enough to turn the tiller though it wouldn't have mattered with both ships drifting gently in the current. "I couldn't do that to you, Rowan. We go too far back. I'd hate to damage the past with a clouded future." Rowan grunted in surprise.

"You actually think there do be anything left to our friendship, Cass?" he asked bemusedly. "Well, I'm happy to tell ya, ya thieving bastard, *that* ship sailed long ago." He regretted the comment the moment he spoke it. The last thing Rowan needed was to give Cass another excuse to walk away with his scale.

Cass marched back to Rowan, black boots shining with each ominous step.

"I'm going to allow you to make up your unpaid taxes right here, right now," Cass said, his voice oily as leviathan fat. "I'll mark it down in my ledgers," he said making a flicking motion as if he were actually signing the ledger already. "Right here on your ship for you to witness. With your signature and mine, it will be as binding as anything under the law can be. The only thing is, I will need payment before I leave your deck." The smile that formed on Cass's face said everything words couldn't.

Silence hung about them like a stale breeze, thick, putrid and filled with tension. Rowan stared daggers into Cass's eyes. He put into it all the hatred he could muster.

"Other than that, Rowan," Cass said looking down at the scale, "you are as destitute as a beggar *without* a tin cup. At least, here on the ship you are. I know you've amassed a great deal of wealth."

Rowan looked down at the scale in his hand. The faces of his fallen crewmen he'd seen earlier in the polished gold returned, flashing one after another. He'd only had the memento for just a few tense minutes and already it had become his third most dear possession. That, and the crewmen still living in his employ. *But can I give it up,* he thought, feeling not just physical weight but also the emotional weight of the scale in his hands. It was either that or surrender the ship to the last man he'd ever want to have her. But would that be the worst thing?

"Why now, Cass?" Rowan asked. "How bout I let ya arrest me and take me back to Manks? I got plenty of gold. I can have Shannon bring yer damn taxes once we get home."

"I'm sorry, Rowan, but that's not going to work for me— though I have no problem arresting you if that's what you want," Cass said laughing. That gurgling pelican was a dagger to Rowan's heart. Law be damned, Rowan knew he was caught sideways in the trough. If he let Cass arrest him to pay the man back later, he knew he wouldn't receive the scale in return. It would go to the smelters and the ore would be separated from the carbon and iron to figure out the exact weight of gold that was taken. It would never be whole again. He'd get back an equal amount to what was taken, but he could kiss the scale goodbye and he'd have lost a lot of time going through the whole rigmarole. The answer was simple, but it sure wasn't easy.

He handed over the scale. It landed regretfully in Cass's greedy hands, leaving an empty pit in Rowan's stomach. For a moment he thought he'd be sick.

"Good man," Cass said with a wicked smile. "Smartest move you've ever made." Cass turned away from him and descended the steps, his high-pitched, pelican-like chuckle wafting back to Rowan's ears. He wanted to chase after the man and strangle him. Snap his neck. Take his scale back. Burn down the *Cutlass* and all the men on board, but instead he stood there and watched Cass cross over to his own ship. He was back in minutes with a ledger and a quill-tipped pen. Luckily for Cass, Rowan's rage had tempered by the time he returned.

"Your signature?" Cass asked, holding out the ledger.

Rowan took the quill and dipped the tip in a jar of squid ink, but before he signed, he looked up at his old partner and pointed the quill in his face. "I'll get this scale back, Cass. You mark my words."

"Sure, Rowan," Cass said with a bemused smile. "Whatever you say."

Rowan signed his name.

After letting the ink settle into the fibrous paper, Cass snapped the ledger shut with a winning smile. Victory was Cass's and he knew it. Rowan's life was signed away right there. A part of him would always be missing. He saw no circumstance in which he could ever get the scale back.

"Undoubtedly," Cass said, his voice light and friendly, "the gold on this scale is worth more than what you owe the throne. When I get back to Manks, I'll melt it down and weigh out your part. You can collect your share whenever you get back. Sound good?" Without waiting for a response from Rowan, Cass turned around and snapped his fingers. The half dozen Kingmen that came aboard fell into line behind him like a flock of ducklings and followed their mother back to the ship.

PART SEVEN

There's a balance good men seek to achieve, a destination too few have ventured far enough to find. This confluence between ambition and power is ideologically a holy achievement to many. But those whose morals have become murky cannot see this junction between the two, and the resulting consequences almost always become tempestuous.

—Fergus Culkin, captain of the Domnall, *leviathan ship of the first class, personal ship of the king*

CHAPTER SIXTEEN

Cassidy watched the *Slayer of the Sea* tack starboard to catch the wind. What a ridiculous name for a ship. And three hulls? He remembered the day Rowan came up with the idea. It sounded so absurd. His skepticism was short lived, however, when construction was finally completed and the vessel's maiden voyage proved him wrong. Eating his own words dug at him, tying his stomach in knots.

Rowan always had a preference for dramatics. It was, in part, what made him such a damn good captain. That, and the fact that Rowan was probably the wealthiest fisherman in all the isles of Manks. There were plenty of folks richer than Rowan, but most were politicians or black-market slavers.

Still, Rowan was different. Different in that he came by his wealth honestly. That fact alone drove Cassidy crazy since he'd broken countless laws trying to put the leviathan hunter behind bars. It was so frustrating watching him succeed in everything he wanted day after day, year after year, while Cassidy struggled to rise up through the ranks of the military. Why couldn't anything come easy for *him?*

If only he could have gotten under Rowans skin a little more. Trying to gall the man was purely an exercise in selfishness that didn't quite land the reaction he wanted. Cassidy didn't see him panic or lose his composure with his threat of taxes, at least, not at first. Not until...

Turning over the plate sized leviathan scale in his hands, Cassidy marveled at the amount of gold woven into it. It was incredibly heavy. In gold weight alone, this single scale would buy him his own hundred-foot luxury yacht. One that could closely match even that of the king. He couldn't have one made brand new. He'd buy an older ship and have it renovated.

He shook his head clear of selfish dreams. What was he thinking? He couldn't let thoughts like that grow too powerful. Material possessions were nothing compared to power.

Yes. That would be far more valuable than an old boat.

"Time's up, *Lieutenant* Commander," a man said from behind him. Cassidy flinched in surprise and turned from his vigil to see the ship's commander standing behind him. "Take off the captain's jacket," Nolan was a tall, slender man with penetrating green eyes. Coincidentally, he was also the finest swordsman in the fleet and second only to the Captain. Nolan's hand floated near the gold-laced hilt of his cutlass. Cassidy's mouth went dry. "You had yer fun, though I doubt Captain Donchaad believed you'd actually been given command of this ship."

Nolan's comment stung, though Cassidy didn't think the swordsman's assumption was accurate. Rowan had given Cassidy deference without any kind of questioning behavioral cues. No, Rowan had believed or he never would have turned over the scale.

"Doesn't matter," Cassidy replied, flipping open the jacket and sliding it down off his arms. It landed on the deck at Cassidy's feet. "The captain can have his jacket. He can have this ship, and he can even have my respect." Though any man that could sleep through the afternoon, bombed out on whiskey, should deserve none of it. He turned and walked away from the commander, eager to return to his private chambers. "I've already got the only thing I need," he mumbled, holding up the scale with a wry smirk on his face.

"That do be the property of the king," Nolan said, following after him.

"It 'do be' my own personal property," Cassidy said mockingly over his shoulder.

"But the taxes, the forms." Nolan reached out and snatched the sheaf of papers tucked under Cassidy's arm and flipped through them. Cassidy rounded on him.

"A ruse, Nolan," he sneered, swiping back the pages. "Only a ruse." Honestly, the man may have been a brilliant swordsman, but he lacked the intelligence that would have made him truly dangerous. "A tactic I've learned from our dear captain. If there's something you want, create whatever truth's necessary for you to take it. Rowan's not behind on his taxes, if anything he's paid out more than his share. If he hadn't been so scared of me taking this treasure away from him he'd have thought clearly enough to see it."

Continuing on his way, Cassidy passed by the men he'd brought with him on his inspection of the *Slayer of the Sea*. They nodded and smiled wryly. Cassidy held up the scale and winked. Each man was loyal to him, complicit in many of his past crimes and in so doing, were very rich men. He didn't need to worry about his plunder being taken from him by the captain or any other man on the *Cutlass*. A mutiny would not be too far-fetched an idea. Both Nolan and their drunken captain would be easy to kill.

Well, maybe not Nolan.

But the one thing Cassidy wasn't going to tell his men was that they'd never see an ounce of gold from *this* particular treasure. He'd definitely pay them, but with money from his own coffers. Their loyalty was not something he could let wash away from just any storm.

And then, suddenly, he realized the best use of such an item.

He would give it to the king. As crazy as that sounded, he would. And in so doing, earn the respect of the man as well as a seat on his political and military council. With that power, he could command whatever ship he wanted, hunt down whoever he wanted, and exact revenge however he saw fit. Rowan Donchaad would then be just a rich civilian and Cassidy Alby would be a military commander with all the weight of the king behind him.

He passed through the members of his private crew, losing Nolan who was unwilling to push through men that clearly didn't fear him. Cassidy turned around to see the man backing slowly away.

"Give the captain my regards, Nolan," Cassidy said with a wave and a smirk. He was down the companion ladder in seconds, past the many rows of hammocks in the forecastle to the door of his private chambers. Cassidy inserted a small key in the lock, turned it until the lock clicked, and shouldered open the door.

The room was slightly dim. A small, ovate window on the back wall let in ample light for Cassidy to see by.

It was a small room, with very little to tell anyone who occupied it. In the corner was a fold up desk and an empty chair with a single chest between it and a frame bed with twin down mattresses. Cassidy smiled when he looked at his meager belongings, and set the scale down on the desk that creaked under its weight.

He still couldn't believe it was actually his. This scale would give him the power he lusted after. Would give him everything he desired.

He wanted the power to strip his old friend of everything

he held dear. He wanted the man's ship. He wanted his crew. He wanted his wealth. But more than all that, much more than that, Cassidy wanted his old partner, Rowan Donchaad, to covet *him*. He wanted Rowan to feel inferior for once.

Looking at the massive leviathan scale he'd stolen, a heady sense of excitement swelled inside him, filling him to almost bursting. He wanted to shout, to scream, to celebrate his victory. His spine shivered as the hair on his arms tingled with goose bumps.

This scale was a start. In truth, it was more than that. Much more.

It was a spark to light the powder keg that would sink Rowan's entire world.

CHAPTER
SEVENTEEN

As the mighty Privileged vessel pulled away from the *Slayer of the Sea* and shrank further and further into the distance, Rowan sensed a presence beside him. He knew who it had to be. The footsteps were far too quiet.

"Marek? Where ya been, lad?" He didn't remember seeing the boy the entire time Cass had detained his ship.

"In the gull's nest, sir. I figured I'd take Jannon's spot while he was down here watching the Kingmen rob us blind." Marek spat in defiance. The boy's contempt toward Cassidy's men brought a smile to Rowan's face. He'd probably never had anything stolen from him before, making this a gesture of support for his captain. Rowan found the gesture a small bit of comfort. He really was a good lad. Good initiative as well.

"I don't know what ya saw from up there," Rowan said gazing up at the topmost mast. He didn't know the lad had such a good head for heights. "But I think I just lost the greatest treasure of my life today." Rowan bowed his head and gently kicked over a nearby bucket. Sea water spilled across the deck.

"That scale, sir?" Marek asked, stealing a glance at the departing *Cutlass*. "The one with all the gold in it?"

"That do be the one," Rowan said, ruffling the lad's hair.

He was surprised how much the boy had seen and heard, stowed away in the gull's nest. Remarkable. "More'n likely I'll never get it back, or find one so large to replace it." He put a hand on Marek's shoulder and walked him to the starboard rail. Both Belinus and Belinos were at their peak, shining hot and bright on a glassy sea that sparkled like a field of multi-colored gems.

"The ocean is a big place, Marek," he said inhaling deeply. "Full of big leviathans. If we found one once then mayhap we could find another just as big." *If a second beast even exists.*

"Well, sir, that's really what I came down here to tell you," Marek said gazing up at him.

Rowan looked at Marek in confusion. "Tell me what, lad?" His stomach started to churn.

"I saw a steam cloud. On the other side of the ship," he said, gesturing over his shoulder. "Mannix told me once that the biggest Devourers in the ocean are solitary creatures. I can't imagine the leviathan that attacked us allowing another one anywhere close to it. That means it would have to be the same one, wouldn't it?"

Rowan could hardly believe his ears. Was this boy telling the truth? *Abandinus, please let it be so!*

"Marek?"

"Yes, Captain?"

"Next time ya see a steam cloud," Rowan chided, a thrill coming over him, "don't bother come'n down to tell me. Just start shout'n fer all yer worth!" With a wink, Rowan turned from his cabin boy and ran for the bridge as fast as his feet could carry him.

But ascending the ladder to the wheel where Berit waited his command to turn and follow the plume, Rowan slowed, a strange warmth spreading through him. It settled into every pore of his body and caused his skin to tingle in an unfamiliar, calming way.

"Captain?" Berit asked, seeming confused by Rowan's sudden change in behavior. "Do there be something amiss? Did the boy tell you what he saw?"

Rowan looked out over the sea. The steam cloud may not have even been visible, but in his mind he could see a micro plume way out in the distance. *A Devourer.* There was only a one in a million chance he'll ever find the creature, or another to match it, ever again. He spied the eyeglass where he'd thrown it on the deck, and picked it up, looking toward the cloud. The image through the lens was crisp and clear. Rowan grunted in surprise when he made out the plume rising off the sea. He lowered the glass to look at the deck boss, remembering he'd asked him a question.

"No, Berit," he replied, his body humming with excitement and warmth. Rowan patted his chest and arms, exploring the new sensation. "Nothing do be amiss. I just... Go ahead and set course."

"Aye, captain." Berit saluted, a slight pinch to his eyes. Rowan could tell he didn't quite believe him. It was one of the reason's Berit made such a good leader. He could read behavior better than reading a book.

Rowan opened the door to his cabin and crossed over to Aifric still lying on the makeshift cot. Somebody had lifted him back onto the trunks. He could see the man's chest slowly rising and falling with every breath. A cool, wet cloth rested on Aifric's brow. Outside he could hear Berit ordering the crewmen.

Rowan knelt at his first mate's side and lifted the cloth away, feeling the man's temperature, afraid to find him still burning with fever. When their skin met, a gentle coolness greeted him.

Abandinus preserve us!

A sudden increase in the pounding pressure of his blood fueled a slight panic inside him. Quickly, he touched Aifric's cheeks. Cool. He felt his neck and chest. Both were cool. He yelled to Berit through the open door.

"What is it Captain?"

"It's Aifric! What did Marek do when he brought up the wet towels?"

"Is Aifric okay?" Berit asked, looking in from the doorway.

"Just answer the damn question, Berit. What did the boy do?" Rowan flung the sheet down to Aifric's waist, exposing his bare chest. He placed his hand over Aifric's heart. A steady beat met Rowans palm and he pulled his hand away in shock. He ran his hands over his hair, pulling stray strands back away from his face. He sat back on his heels, staring in wonder.

"I don't think he did anything, Captain," Berit said, walking over to stand behind him. "Nothing out of the ordinary, anyway. Just wiped him down with that wet rag. Same as anybody would'a done, I suppose."

Rowan pressed an ear to Aifric's chest listening to his heart. He touched his own chest to compare their rhythms. Still steady.

"Did those Privileged bastards do something to him when they were in here?" Berit asked, a sudden tenseness in his voice.

"Shush!" Rowan held out a hand to forestall any more noise from the man. Their hearts beat in perfect rhythm. He stood and began pacing his cabin. His bare feet shuffled softly across the worn, polished boards. How could anybody recover this quickly? How? Rowan doubted Doc Samuel had medicine that could act this fast. It seemed to be a... a...

A miracle.

"His fever is gone, Berit," Rowan said, hands on his head in disbelief. "And his heart do be as stable as my own." Rowan lifted away the linen sheet that covered his legs. A pit opened in his stomach when he saw the bloody bandage covering the stump where Aifric's leg used to be. He heard Berit groan.

Hesitantly, unsure if he were making a huge mistake, he found the end of the cloth bandage and began to unwrap the wound. *No fever. Does this mean there do be no infection?*

"Oh, Captain, no," Berit protested. Rowan looked up at the man who had a fist over his mouth and was taking a step back. "You know what, let me get Doc Samuel to do that."

But Rowan ignored him and continued to unwrap the leg. The bloodstains turned a slightly green color the further he went. When the last bit of infection-soaked wrapping fell away he gasped. So did Berit.

"Abandinus preserve and protect us!" they intoned together, staring at the stump of leg. Berit grasped Rowan's arm, hiding slightly behind him.

Where the skin had been stitched together to cover the sawed-off stump of bone, a bright pink scar stood out vibrant and smooth. No stitch remained to be seen. More importantly, there was no infection whatsoever. He looked up at his deck boss in astonishment. Never had he seen the like. Neither had he heard of anything so miraculous. How could a man so near death heal this fast? What caused it? What made the difference?

Then suddenly he knew.

The scale!

It was the only differing factor. He'd heard the myths behind leviathan's supposed magical qualities. The suits they made from leviathan skin could easily be considered magical, but never would he have thought a scale could heal an amputated leg.

Aifric moaned.

CHAPTER
EIGHTEEN

"He's awake, captain!" Berit cried, slapping Rowan on the shoulder.

"Get him some water, Berit. Quick!" Rowan ordered. "Aifric? Can ya hear me?" He abandoned the stump and returned to kneel at Aifric's side once more. Berit disappeared in a flash.

"Rowan?" Aifric's voice rasped like a taut rope pulled over a rail. Rowan expected him to open his eyes fully, but his friend kept them closed.

Aifric slowly turned his head from side to side and gingerly lifted his hand to blindly reach out for him. Rowan clasped it in his. It felt weak, but pleasantly cool. "I'm here, mate. How do ya feel?"

"Like I've been kept awake for a month," Aifric said, rubbing his eyes with his free hand. "I'm so... tired."

"Do you know where you are?" Berit asked, coming into the room. He grasped a wooden cup of water in his hands.

Aifric didn't respond right away.

"Here, mate," Rowan said taking the cup from Berit, "drink some water. Can you sit up?"

Aifric slowly shook his head.

"It's okay," Rowan said. "Here, I'll just pour a little in yer mouth." Rowan was careful not to gag him as he poured and handed the cup back to Berit. After a minute Aifric opened his eyes, blinking away the light.

"On the *Slayer*," Aifric said in response to Berit's question.

"That's right," Rowan said, "we do be on the ship. Good." He motioned for Berit to give him back the cup.

"Leviathan," Aifric mumbled.

Rowan froze.

"You remember?" Rowan asked in astonishment. How he kept feeling surprised by Aifric's recovery was a surprise in itself. What exactly had that scale done to him?

"Yeah," he said, "damn near killed me." Aifric's voice had become slightly less raspy. His recovering strength was starting to show.

Rowan laughed softly, patting Aifric tenderly on the chest. "Indeed," he said. "Damn near killed me too."

Aifric turned his head to the side, locking eyes with Rowan. "Are you... are you hurt?" The concern on Aifric's face brought that warm feeling from before back again.

"No, old friend, just a few bruises is all." As if someone had just lit a candle, Rowan realized he had felt absolutely no discomfort whatsoever. No lingering pain at all, though he knew he'd smashed his face pretty hard. *Stagnation, it'd even knocked me senseless, for Abandinus' sake!*

"Marek!" Aifric suddenly shouted. "Where is he, Rowan? Is Marek alive? Stagnation, he was right next to me when we were—when we— "

"He's okay, Aifric," Rowan said, becoming aware of the ache in his knees. "He's perfectly fine. There no be a scratch on him."

"Can I see him?" Aifric's voice shook with eagerness.

"Berit, can ya get the boy?" Rowan said over his shoulder.

"I'm on it, Captain!" Berit replied, exiting the cabin, a spring to his step.

A few minutes later Marek walked slowly in, his footsteps short, hesitant.

"I'll give you two a minute." Rowan walked to the doorway and paused, looking back. "Aifric," he took a long breath, "I'm glad ya do be alive old friend. I'll be need'n yer guidance in the years to come." Rowan smiled warmly, even though he doubted Aifric could see, and was out the door.

He relieved Berit who had returned to the wheel. Rowan needed a moment or two of silence to take in everything that just happened with Aifric and the scale. He fingered the king spoke, the longest spoke on the wheel, with its polished brass covering. A nail holding it in place was starting to work its way free. Rowan pressed his thumb on it until it left an indentation in his skin. Everything, it seemed, left a mark.

This was his fault.

Everything. The death. The injuries. The loss. All his fault.

He saw the leviathan under the water and knew he was out of his league, but his greed had turned away common sense when he saw the glisten of gold, and his desire to have it all led his crew to disaster.

They all could have died. Only a miracle had kept most alive. *What would have happened to the ship if I had died too? Stagnation, what would have happened to my baby girl? Raised without a father?* For the first time, the thought of her cerulean eyes nearly brought him to tears. *How could I have been so callous to leave without seeing her, holding her?* She was the last remnant of the woman he loved more than anything in this world. A living part of her. Stagnation, Aifric was right. He'd been a fool.

The door to his cabin opened and Marek emerged,

smiling down at the deck. His shoulders seemed broader, and Rowan could have sworn the boy looked taller.

"How's yer uncle, lad?"

"Asleep, sir," Marek said looking up. A gleam of hope sparkled in his brown eyes.

"Good, good. What did he say," Rowan asked, "if ya don't mind me ask'n?"

"He asked about the crew," he said, folding his hands under his arms, "if anybody had—you know."

"And what did ya tell him?" Rowan asked, slightly adjusting the tiller. The compass started drifting away from the needle.

"I... I told him everybody made it back safe," Marek said, looking directly into Rowan's eyes. Was the lad looking for approval? "I know it was a lie, but I didn't want him to worry, ya know?"

"Ya did the right thing, lad." Rowan grasped the boy's shoulder, pulling him in for a side-hug. It felt awkward, but he hoped it would comfort him. Rowan wasn't used to things like that, having never known what fathers normally did in these situations.

"What now, Captain?" Marek asked, stepping back from the hug a moment later. "Do we go after the leviathan? Do we get our revenge?" Marek smacked a fist into his palm.

Rowan looked down into the boy's eyes and was surprised at the passion that burned there, hot and fierce. *Stagnation, he looks a lot like me!* This disaster should have been more than a child his age could handle, thought it would have scared him off the sea entirely. But it appeared to have done the opposite.

Abandinus preserve the lad. He can't end up like me. I can't let him.

"No, Marek," he said, turning fully back to the wheel. He

checked the compass, adjusted their bearing, and looked out over the water.

"But why, Captain?" Marek asked, moving to the rail and looking in the direction of the plume. "It's not *too* far away. I can remember the exact direction the leviathan went." Marek looked up at the main sail, billowed and taut. "With as much wind as we have we can be caught up in no time." A slight downturn to Marek's eyebrows gave away the lad's reserve. Rowan could tell he wasn't entirely sure what he said was true. Marek was still so new to all of this.

"You ask why, lad?" he said, thinking it over. Rowan had several reasons for not chasing after the beast, least of which was the unlikelihood of the leviathan staying close to the surface for so long. It'd die from the heat of its own body if it didn't dive soon.

"Because there's men on board this ship that need to heal," he finally said. "And a man has to know when enough is enough."

Marek's shoulders slumped.

"But more importantly," Rowan said, anchoring the wheel in place and walking over to Marek's side. Together they leaned against the starboard rail and looked out over the water. Belinus was just beginning to dip beyond the horizon, setting the sea ablaze with fire. "Because a pair of blue eyes need to meet their father."

Marek looked up at him with furrowed, questioning brows. Rowan laughed, knowing his last comment was somewhat confusing, and ruffled the boy's short hair.

Rowan spent so much of his life narrowly focused on a single purpose. Even back when he and Birgitta were together, before that storm hit them in the bay, she was secondary to his single-minded objective.

The hunt. Only the hunt. It was all that had ever truly mattered to him. He knew now that was a mistake.

But Rowan wasn't ready to give up the hunt entirely. In truth, he doubted he ever could. It was too much a part of what made him who he was. But maybe, just maybe, he could spend a little more time at home, slay a few less monsters. Perhaps he could finally learn how to be a father.

ABOUT THE AUTHOR

Beau Peterson is a fan of all things fantasy and science fiction. As a small business owner, he listens to a crazy amount of audiobooks that help him keep his sanity. He also enjoys the great outdoors, watching and participating in sports, and of course *writing*! He lives in Utah with his beautiful wife and their four sons who, of course, never give him any reason to stress.

This has been an
Immortal Production

www.ingramcontent.com/pod-product-compliance
Lightning Source LLC
Chambersburg PA
CBHW050149110726
47898CB00008B/2732